Chapter 1

When I woke at six-thirty, Jack was already up. I eventually found him in the lounge.

"Be careful! Don't tread on those," he cautioned, when he saw me at the door. The floor was covered in bowling shirts, as were the table, sofa and chairs. "I didn't realise I had so many."

"I'm glad you're having a clear out. It's certainly not before time. How many bowling shirts can one man possibly need?"

"I'm not throwing any of these away." He looked appalled at the idea. "I'm just planning my wardrobe for the rest of the season's matches."

"Please tell me you're not serious?"

"I'm deadly serious. There are prizes at stake."

"How can the shirt you wear have any bearing on your performance?"

"I'm not talking about prizes for the bowling. We're already well ahead in the league, so that's pretty much in the bag. But there's still the prizes for best dressed team and individual to be awarded."

"You do realise that on a scale of nought to sad, this scores an eleven, don't you?"

"Your problem, Jill, is that you don't have any hobbies or interests. You really should find something that you could feel passionate about, other than your work."

"Such as?"

"Ten-pin bowling?"

"Boring."

"Ballroom dancing?"

"Tedious."

"There must be something you enjoy? Didn't you used to have any hobbies or interests when you were a kid?"

"There were the beanies."

"I meant some kind of activity?"

"Not really. Activity was more Kathy's thing. I was more a *laze around the house* kind of a kid."

"In that case, I'm going to make it my mission to find something that you can throw yourself into, something that will get you out of the house."

"That's really not necessary."

"Nonsense. You'll thank me later."

I very much doubted that.

By the time I'd showered and dressed, Jack had cleared away his collection of bowling shirts, and was staring out of the front window.

"The balaclava twins are beyond weird," he said.

"What are they up to now?"

"About ten minutes ago, the guy came out of his house, and walked up the street and then back down again. A couple of minutes later, the woman did the same thing."

"Were they looking at our house?"

"I don't think so; I'm not sure what they were doing."

I had a horrible feeling that the balaclava twins were the brother and sister witchfinders: Vinnie and Minnie Dreadmore. The only thing I knew about them was that they both had grey hair, which might explain why our weird neighbours insisted on wearing balaclavas all the time. Somehow, I needed to get a look at them when they weren't wearing their headgear.

On his way out of the door, Jack hesitated. "You haven't forgotten we're going to Kathy's tonight, have you?"

"No, of course I haven't." Even though I'd tried very hard to.

"And don't forget to get them a present and a card."

"Why do I have to do it?"

"Because she's your sister."

"I might not have time."

"You'll have to find time. It's not like you didn't know it was their anniversary. I've been reminding you for weeks now."

"Okay, I'll get them a present."

"And a card."

"Yes, and a card." Sheesh, my life wasn't my own. "I'll meet you at Kathy's then, shall I?"

"Aren't you coming home to get changed first?"

"What for? It's only Kathy and Peter."

"It's their wedding anniversary. We should get dressed up."

"But it's only Kathy and Peter."

"I'm coming home to change. I thought I'd wear my new grey suit."

"But it's only—Oh, okay then. I'll come home and get changed too, but if they're both dressed in T-shirts and trackie bottoms, it'll be your fault."

Before setting out for work, I double checked that I had the syringes of Brewflower in my bag. Yvonne's warning about the witchfinders was still ringing in my ears. The three who had been assigned to kill me were the best in the business, so I couldn't afford to let my guard down, even for a minute. Although I was fairly sure that I'd identified two of them, I still had The Rose to worry about. It was at times like this that I occasionally yearned for my old life—the one I had before I discovered I was a witch. At least then, there weren't people on every street corner, trying to kill me.

When I stepped out of the house, I was greeted by a seahorse and a carrot. Tony and Clare, our next-door neighbours, were obsessed with cosplay, and seemed to attend a different convention every weekend.

"You guys have got me stumped this time. I can't imagine which convention would include seahorses *and* carrots."

"In actual fact, Jill, these costumes are for two different cons," Tony the carrot, said.

"I love AquaCon," the seahorse said. "It's one of my favourites. Unfortunately, this year, it falls on the same weekend as Tony's favourite con."

"I've always loved VegCon," the carrot said. "We tried to decide which one we should attend, but couldn't agree, so for the first time ever, we're going to different cons this weekend. You and Jack are welcome to come to VegCon, if you like? There's any number of wonderful costumes to choose from. You'd make a great cabbage, Jill."

"Don't listen to him," the seahorse said. "If you're both free this weekend, you should come to AquaCon. You'd look good as a—"

"Mermaid?" I suggested.

"I was going to say a lobster."

"Don't waste your time with those boring fishes, Jill," the carrot said. "Vegetables are where it's at."

"Rubbish!" the seahorse objected. "Who cares about a few stupid vegetables?"

While the seahorse and carrot were still squabbling, I

managed to sneak away.

***

Mr Ivers was all alone in the toll booth, and he didn't look happy.

"Good morning, Mr Ivers."

"No, it isn't. My elbows are giving me gyp."

"Where's Cole?"

I'd recently been instrumental in bringing Cole the troll over from Candlefield, to work in the toll booth. With his expertise of collecting money on bridges, he'd been a natural.

"He left." Mr Ivers frowned.

"But he's only been here five minutes. I thought he'd settled into the job well."

"He had. Too well. That's the problem. When I was back at the main office, I made the mistake of mentioning how well my new assistant was doing. The next thing I knew, Cole had been tempted away by an offer from another toll booth operator. He offered him twice what I could afford to pay."

"Good for Cole."

Mr Ivers glared at me.

"But disappointing for you, obviously."

"I don't suppose you know of anyone else with Cole's level of experience, do you?"

"I'm afraid not."

"If my elbows don't improve, I may have to look for a different line of work. Do you need any help? I could see myself as a private investigator."

"I'm afraid not, and besides, it takes years of

experience."

"Really? You seem to muddle along okay."

***

"I have amazing news," Mrs V said. She was obviously excited about something because she could barely sit still. "Armi popped the question last night."

"What question?"

"He asked me to marry him, of course. It came completely out of the blue. We get along like a house on fire, but I never expected this—not even in my wildest dreams."

"I take it you said yes?"

"Of course."

"I'm absolutely thrilled for you." I gave her a hug.

"I want you and Jules to be my bridesmaids."

"Me? A bridesmaid?"

"It would make me so happy. I've already spoken to Jules. I called her first thing. You will do it, won't you, Jill?"

"Err—yeah, of course. I'd love to."

Winky was on the sofa. "What's the old bag lady so excited about?"

"Mrs V is getting married."

"Don't be daft." He laughed. "Who'd have that old—"

"That's enough of that. Mrs V is a wonderful woman. Armi is lucky to have her."

"Is he blind? Or just stupid?"

"Neither. He's very much in love."

"It's hardly worth them bothering."

"What do you mean?"

"Well, it can't be long before she'll be pushing up the daisies."

"What a horrible thing to say. Sometimes, I despair of you."

"I'm only saying what everyone else will be thinking. When is this wedding?"

"I don't know. She didn't actually say, but she has asked me to be her bridesmaid."

"You?" He laughed even louder. "A bridesmaid? Do me a favour."

"Jules is going to be one too."

"Does that mean you'll be standing next to her in the photographs? Oh dear."

"What do you mean, *oh dear*?"

"Well, she's young. And pretty. And you're—"

"I hope you aren't expecting any salmon today, or for the rest of the year."

My first appointment of the day wasn't for another thirty minutes, so I busied myself with important P.I. admin work.

Winky jumped onto my desk. "I'm sorry to interrupt your paperclip sorting."

"It's no good begging for salmon, not after what you said just now."

"Nah, I'm not bothered about the salmon."

"Aren't you feeling well?"

"Peggy has got me on a diet." He sighed. "I just wanted to remind you that Socks will be popping by later."

"What do you mean: *remind me*? This is the first I've heard of it."

"Oh dear, that memory of yours."

"Don't give me that. You never mentioned that Socks would be coming."

"He's only popping in for a few minutes, that's all."

"It had better be no longer than that. You know how I feel about your brother."

"He's off on holiday, and he's asked me to look after something for him while he's away. Probably a plant."

***

Mrs V came through to my office, and dropped a brochure on my desk. "I hope you don't mind, but I just nipped out to get this."

How could I object when I didn't even pay her?

"Wedding Dreams? Is that the shop next door to the fried chicken takeaway?"

"That's the one, dear. The woman who runs it is lovely. She said I can get ten percent off my first purchase."

"That's nice." It was probably to compensate for the smell of spicy chicken wings on the stock.

"Look at this dress. I thought something like this would be ideal for you and Jules."

"It's pink."

"My favourite colour."

"And frilly."

"Lovely, isn't it?"

"That bow is rather large."

"You and Jules will look lovely in these. I can't wait to show it to her."

"I've been thinking, Mrs V. Might it be better to have Jules and Lules as your bridesmaids? They are—"

"No. I barely know Lules. You do want to do it, don't you, Jill?"

I was desperate to say no, but it would have been like kicking a kitten.

"Of course I do." I glanced at my watch. "My first appointment should have been here ten minutes ago. They must be running late."

"The Bradleys? Oh dear, I'd completely forgotten about them. They're in the outer office."

"Right. You'd better show them in, then."

"I'd make a better receptionist than the old bag lady," Winky said when Mrs V went to collect the Bradleys.

"She's just excited about the wedding. What time is Socks coming?"

"I don't know."

"He'd better not come sailing through the window while I'm with my clients. I'm not sure how I'd explain away a microlight-flying cat."

Thomas Bradley was tall, slim and very loud. Georgina, his wife, was petite and mouse-like. They both looked to be in their mid-forties.

"How can I help you?" I posed the question to them both, but I wasn't too surprised when he was the one who answered.

"My brother, Stephen, was murdered ten years ago. It was the anniversary of his death the day before yesterday."

"I see. I take it that his murderer was never brought to justice?"

"That's right, which is why we're here today. After all of this time, it's obvious that the police are never going to find the murderer. We hope that you can."

"Can you talk me through what happened ten years ago?"

He turned to his wife, "Maybe you should start, darling."

The mouse looked unsure, but eventually found her voice. "Stephen was working late, which wasn't particularly unusual. When it got to eleven o'clock, and he wasn't back, I decided to go to bed, but when I woke the next morning, he still hadn't come home."

"Sorry, I'm a little confused." I turned to Thomas Bradley. "I thought Stephen was your brother?"

"Sorry, we should have explained. Stephen was my brother; he and Georgina were man and wife at the time he was murdered."

"I see."

"After Stephen's death, Georgina and I found comfort in each other's company. We didn't plan for it to happen, but slowly and surely, we fell in love. We were married about five years ago."

"I see. Sorry for interrupting. You were telling me about the day that Stephen died."

She continued, "When I realised Stephen hadn't come home, I became very worried. Although he often worked late, he never stayed out all night. I called his mobile phone, but it went to voicemail. I called his office number, but there was no reply. I was just about to call the police when they turned up at my door. Stephen's PA had found him dead in his office. He'd been beaten to death."

"What can you tell me about the police investigation?"

"There isn't much to tell." Thomas took over the story. "The murder weapon was a large metal paperweight from

Stephen's desk. No unusual fingerprints or DNA were found at the scene, and the CCTV didn't throw up any useful leads."

"What did your husband do for a living, Mrs Bradley?"

Before she could answer, Thomas jumped in again, "We were partners in an advertising agency. West Star, you've probably heard of it?"

"No, I can't say I have."

"We're now the largest in Washbridge, but back then we were a much smaller outfit."

"Did your husband do or say anything just prior to his death that gave you cause to worry?"

"No." Georgina shook her head. "In fact, he was very upbeat because of the possibility of a takeover, which would have meant a large windfall. He was already planning how we'd spend it."

"What happened with the takeover bid?" I addressed the question to Thomas Bradley.

"It fell through, as it turned out."

"Is the business still based in the same offices as ten years ago?"

"We're in the same building, but we've taken more space."

"I'd like to see the offices at some point. I assume that can be arranged?"

"Of course."

"Georgina, where were you living when your husband died?"

"In the same house where Thomas and I live today."

"Right. Maybe I could come and talk to you there, later in the week?"

"Of course."

Twenty minutes later, we wrapped up the meeting, and the Bradleys went on their way. Fortunately, we hadn't been interrupted by the feline microlight pilot.

"Any news on when Socks is going to arrive, Winky?" He was so engrossed with his phone that he didn't hear me, so I shouted, "Winky!"

"Hold on. I can't afford to miss this."

Five minutes later, he put the phone down.

"What was so fascinating that you couldn't drag yourself away?"

"Don't you realise what day it is?"

I shrugged.

"It's Ginger Monday."

"It's what?"

"You've heard of Black Friday, I take it?"

"Of course. It's when perfectly sane people go crazy, and buy tons of stuff they don't really need."

"Ginger Monday is the feline equivalent of Black Friday."

"What have you bought? Something totally useless, no doubt."

"Not at all. I've been meaning to buy one of these for ages."

"Really? What is it?"

"It'll be invaluable."

"So, what is it?"

"A paw-spa."

At that, I cracked up.

"What's so funny about a paw-spa?"

Chapter 2

Aunt Lucy phoned to ask me to go over to Candlefield; she sounded excited, but wouldn't say why over the phone. I magicked myself straight there, and found her in the lounge, having a cup of tea with Amber.

"Tea, Jill?" Aunt Lucy stood up.

"No, thanks. I've not long since had a drink. Where's Pearl?"

"She's in Cuppy C," Amber said. "I've just been for a check-up, so I thought I might as well drop in on Mum on the way back."

"Is everything okay with you and the baby?"

"Yeah. All good."

"Tell Jill your news," Aunt Lucy said.

"William and I have decided on names for the baby."

"Already? You aren't letting the grass grow. What have you chosen?"

"Because we don't know if it's a boy or a girl yet, we thought it would be nice to choose two names that rhymed."

"Err—right?" It was good to know that Amber's pregnancy hadn't affected her craziness.

"So, we chose Phil for a boy, and if it's a little girl—"

"Jill?"

"No. Lil, short for Lily. What do you think?"

"Very nice."

"You won't tell Pearl, will you? You know what she's like; she'll steal our ideas."

"I won't say anything."

Amber finished her drink. "I suppose I'd better get back or Pearl will be on my back." She gave Aunt Lucy a kiss.

"Love you, Mum. See you later, Jill."

"You sounded excited on the phone," I said, once Amber had left.

"I am. Lester and I might be moving to a new house."

"I thought you liked it here?"

"I do. This is a lovely house, but it's time for a change. We've been talking about it for a while, and now that he's in a steady job with a regular wage, there's nothing holding us back."

"Do you have any idea where you'll go?"

"We've already found somewhere."

"You didn't hang around."

"To be honest, we weren't actually looking for a house at the time. We'd just been out for a meal when we spotted the for-sale sign. It's a darling little cottage with a thatched roof, and a beautiful garden."

"It sounds fantastic. I'd love to see it."

"I don't want to jinx it, so I'd rather not take you there until our offer is accepted."

"Have you already made an offer?"

"Yes, Lester did it earlier today. We're just waiting to hear."

"Fingers crossed for you."

"Thanks, Jill. You won't mention this to your grandmother, will you?"

"It's not like you can keep it a secret. I think even Grandma will notice when you move out."

"I know, but I don't want to tell her until the contract is signed. She's bound to give me plenty of grief, and I'd rather not face that before I have to."

"I won't say a word, I promise. Is the new house far from here?"

"No, not far at all."

"I suppose I'd better be getting back. Keep me posted on the house front, won't you?"

"Of course, but before you go, Barry wanted a quick word with you."

"Do you know what it's about?"

"He's got a bee in his bonnet, I'm afraid. I'll let him tell you all about it."

As soon as I walked into the room, Barry came charging over, and jumped up at me.

"Jill! I've got big news!"

"Hi, boy. Get down before you mark my top."

"I'm going to be a star!"

"Can't you take this dog out of here?" Hamlet said. "He's been driving me crazy all morning with his latest madcap scheme. How am I ever supposed to get any reading done?"

Hamlet was even grumpier than usual. He probably still hadn't forgiven me for covering him in flea powder.

"Come on, Barry, let's go out onto the landing." I led the way out of the room, and closed the door behind me, to give Hamlet a little respite. "Okay, what's this all about?"

"I'm going to be a supermodel, Jill."

"I don't know what you mean."

"Look." From somewhere in his fur, he produced a small business card, and handed it to me.

The card read: *Scott Basset, Pooch First - Model Agency.*

"Where did you get this?"

"A man gave it to your auntie when we were in the park. He said I was a handsome dog, and would do well on TV. He said you should phone him if you're interested."

"I'm not sure this is a good idea, Barry."

"Please, Jill. I want to strut my stuff on the dogwalk."

"I'll need to think about it."

"Pretty please. I really want to do this."

"Okay, I'll give them a call later to find out more about the agency."

"You're the best, Jill." He jumped up again, and began to lick my face.

Aunt Lucy was waiting for me when I went back downstairs.

"He's told you, I take it?"

"Yeah. He seems very keen. What was the guy like who gave you the card?"

"He's a vampire. I didn't even notice him until he approached us, but he seemed very taken by Barry. Are you going to contact him?"

"I don't see how I can say no. Barry would be heartbroken. I'll see what I can find out about this agency first, though. I'd better get back to the office. Let me know how you go on with the new house."

***

Back in Washbridge, a small crowd had gathered by the door to my office building. As I got nearer, I could see what was attracting so much attention. A man-sized nail varnish bottle was handing out flyers. As I took one, I caught a glimpse of the man's face through the eye-slot in the costume; it was Nails. The flyer was a twenty percent off voucher for all treatments during Nailed-It's first two days of trading. The nail bar was due to open at midday, and there was already a queue of women on the stairs.

"Hey! You blind or what?" A woman barked at me as I made my way upstairs to my offices. "There's a queue here."

"Yeah. Get in line," her friend joined in.

"I'm not going to the nail bar. My offices are at the top of the stairs."

"You'd better not. I'm watching you."

Mrs V seemed not to have noticed the commotion out on the stairs; she was too engrossed in a magazine. A wedding magazine, needless to say. There were at least a dozen more of them spread across her desk.

"There's so much to plan, Jill," she said, without even looking up.

"Will you have any money left for the wedding after buying this lot?"

"I did go a bit over the top, didn't I? I never realised there were so many."

"Me neither, although I'm pretty sure you're not forced to buy all of them. Incidentally, I see the nail bar is opening today."

"Sorry, dear, what did you say?"

"The nail bar, just down the corridor. It opens later today."

"That's nice. What do you think about the reception?"

"Sorry?"

"Where do you think we should hold the reception?"

"I—err—I'm not really the person to ask. I suppose it depends on how many guests you're planning to invite.

Have you actually set a date yet?"

"Not as such, but we thought sometime next summer. At our age, we can't really afford to hang around."

Just then, I heard sounds coming from in my office. If Socks had crash-landed that microlight of his again, he'd be in for a tongue-lashing.

It wasn't Socks, but the noise *was* feline related.

"Winky? Why are these kittens in my office?"

"These are my nephews and niece. That's Billy, that's Roddy—"

"I'm not Roddy," the black kitten said in a squeaky little voice. "I'm Sammy."

"Sorry. That's Billy, that's *Sammy*, that's Roddy and that's Peaches."

"They're all very sweet, but why are they in my office?"

"Do you recall that I told you Socks wanted me to look after something for a few days? These little darlings are *it*."

"Why didn't you tell me it was kittens?"

"I didn't know until Socks arrived with them in the microlight."

"Don't tell me that he transported all four of them in that death-trap of his."

"It's okay. They were wearing crash helmets. I've put them in your cupboard."

"Hold on. Didn't you say your brother was going on holiday? Are you telling me he's just dumped his kids on you?"

"I don't mind looking after them. I didn't even realise I was an uncle until he turned up with them in tow. He'd never told me."

"That's very generous of you, but I can't have an office full of cats. What will my clients think?"

"You don't have any clients, and besides, you wouldn't throw these poor little mites out onto the street, would you?"

As he spoke, the four kittens all looked at me with big, pitiful eyes.

"I—err—no, of course not. How long has Socks gone away for?"

"Only for a couple of nights. He's going to pick them up on Wednesday."

"Okay. I suppose I'll just have to put up with them until then, but these little bundles of fur are your responsibility. I expect you to keep them in check, and out from under my feet."

"No problem. I've already got them eating out of my paw."

***

It had just turned four o'clock when I remembered that I was supposed to be buying a card and present for Kathy and Peter. If I went home without them, Jack would have my guts for garters.

"I'm calling it a day, Mrs V. I have to do a little shopping."

"Okay, dear. What do you think about limousines? White or black?"

"White, I'd say. Sorry, I have to dash."

I've never understood why it takes some people so long to choose a greetings card. On average, Jack takes at least thirty minutes, but he's lightning fast compared to Kathy.

I could have written a novel in less time than it takes Kathy to pick out a birthday card. I'd long since refused to go into a card shop with her again.

The process is actually very simple: 1) make sure it's for the right occasion (e.g. don't buy a condolences card for someone getting engaged—unless you don't like their partner) and 2) pay as little as possible.

Who are you calling a skinflint? The word you're looking for is frugal.

Trust me, it's a tried and tested method, which is why it took me less than a minute to pick out an anniversary card.

The present was a different matter entirely. What are you supposed to buy someone for their anniversary? I had no idea, which is why I wandered around at least a dozen shops, without anything catching my eye. Jack should have been the one to do this; he was so much better at selecting gifts than I was.

Then I saw it: The perfect present.

"Could I get this gift-wrapped?" I asked the eager assistant.

"Of course, madam. Can I ask what the occasion is?"

"An anniversary."

"Oh? Right."

Mission accomplished.

***

"How do I look?" Jack said; he'd just changed into his new suit.

"Very hot. Why don't we forget the anniversary dinner,

and have our own little 'party' instead?"

"We can't let Kathy and Peter down. They're expecting us. We can have a 'party' when we get back."

"I might not be in the mood, then."

"Aren't you glad you came home to get changed? You look stunning."

"Thank you, kind sir, but that doesn't mean I forgive you for choosing a boring anniversary dinner over me."

His expression suddenly changed to one of panic. "What about the card and present?"

"All in hand. They're in the boot of my car."

We'd tossed a coin to decide which car we'd take, and I'd lost, so not only would I have to put up with a boring anniversary dinner, but I couldn't even have a drink.

Not that I was complaining, obviously.

Although I was never going to admit it, Jack had been right about the dress code. Peter looked very smart in his blue suit; Kathy was wearing a pretty, red dress that I hadn't seen before.

"Happy anniversary." I handed over the card and present.

"Thanks." She gave us both a kiss on the cheek. "Come on through to the lounge, and get a drink."

"Hi, you two." Peter was waiting for us in there. "What's it to be?" He pointed to the line of bottles on the sideboard.

"I'll have whisky on the rocks," Jack said.

"Just a lime and soda for me. I'm driving."

"You should have taken a taxi," Kathy said, as she opened the envelope. "I see Jill chose this card."

"What's wrong with it?"

"Nothing. It's very—err—nice." She placed it on the mantelpiece alongside the others. "How long did it take you to pick it?"

Before I could respond, Peter jumped in, "Why don't you open the present?"

"What is it? It's very big." Kathy began to tear off the paper.

Jack seemed as keen as Kathy and Peter to find out what it was.

"A foot-spa?" Kathy stared at the box. "Err—thanks."

Peter picked up the discarded wrapping paper. "Thanks very much, Jack, Jill."

"Dinner is almost ready," Kathy said. "Shall we go through?"

As we made our way into the dining room, Jack grabbed my hand, and whispered, "A foot-spa? Seriously?"

Kathy had done us proud with the meal. Even I had to admit it was an enjoyable evening; she and Peter were good company.

"I think it's time to tell you our big news," Kathy said, after we'd all finished dessert.

"Are you pregnant again?" It was the first thing to pop into my mind.

"No, I told you, two kids are enough. You've probably realised that I haven't been very happy at Ever for some time. Anyway, we've done our sums, and now that Pete's business is established, I'm going to open a small business of my own."

"You? Run a business?"

"If you can do it, I'm pretty sure I can, and besides, I'll

have Pete to help me with the accounts and stuff like that."

"What kind of business?" Jack asked.

"A bridal shop."

"That's a great idea." Jack nodded his approval.

"Why a bridal shop?" I asked.

"You know how much I love weddings, and people are always going to get married."

"What about the competition?" Jack asked.

"That's another thing that attracted us to the idea. There are only two bridal shops in Washbridge, and neither of them is anything to write home about. We're sure we can do much better."

"I can practically guarantee you one customer," I said.

"Really? About time too. When were you and Jack going to tell us?"

"No, not us. Mrs V is getting married to Armi next year."

"Mrs V? When did this happen?"

"He proposed over the weekend; I found out this morning. She's talked about nothing but the wedding all day."

"When are you planning on opening the shop?" Jack asked.

"We're going to start looking around for suitable premises straight away. Basically, we want to open as soon as possible."

"Have you got a name for the shop?" I said.

"We thought we'd call it Kathy's Bridal Shop."

"Very imaginative. When will you be leaving Ever?"

"The sooner the better because there's lots for us to do before we can open the shop. I'll probably hand in my notice at the end of the week."

"I'm sure Grandma will wish you well."

"I bet. I'm not looking forward to telling her."

When it was time for us to leave, Kathy pulled me to one side.

"How do you fancy a day-trip to Frickle-On-Sea on Wednesday?"

"Jack will be working."

"I meant just you and me. Pete's working too."

Although I'd just taken on the Bradley case, I quite fancied the idea of a day at the seaside. "Okay, why not? Which car shall we take?"

"Let's leave the cars at home. We'll take the coach."

"Good idea. We can both have a drink that way."

"I'll call you tomorrow, and let you have the details."

"Great."

"What are you looking so pleased about?" Jack asked, as I drove home.

"Kathy and I are going to the seaside on Wednesday."

"Huh, it's okay for some. I have to work."

"Never mind. I'll bring you a stick of rock back."

Chapter 3

The previous night's drinking obviously hadn't taken too much of a toll on Jack because he'd already left for work by the time I dragged myself out of bed.

When I got downstairs, I found the note he'd left for me on the kitchen table. It read:

I didn't like to wake you, my beautiful princess. Lots of love and kisses.

It didn't really. It actually read:

We're out of butter. Can you pick some up?

The old romantic.

I took my cornflakes through to the lounge, and noticed a figure across the road. It was one of the balaclava twins, but I couldn't be sure which one. They were staring straight at me, so I waved. As soon as I did that, they turned tail and headed back to their house. This pair were taking weird to a whole new level.

When I took the rubbish outside to the bin, it occurred to me that I hadn't seen Joey, the sand sloth, for a while. With a bit of luck, he'd found another sandpit to live in. After checking that none of the neighbours were around, I called out, "Joey? Are you there?"

"Hi." The little sloth popped his head out of the sand.

Before I could say anything, another sloth appeared.

"Who's that?"

"That's Zoe, my girlfriend. I hope you don't mind, but I told her she could move in with me."

"Hi," Zoe said. "It's very kind of you to let us live here. Finding a free sandpit these days is almost impossible."

"You'll both have to stay out of sight. I can't have you

scaring the neighbours."

"Don't worry, Jill," Joey said. "You won't even know we're here. I promise."

***

On my way to Washbridge, the traffic was moving at a snail's pace. It took me ten minutes to travel no more than a mile, but then I saw the reason for the hold-up. Temporary traffic lights had been erected because of roadworks.

When I finally made it to the front of the queue of cars, I glanced over to see what the workmen were doing.

"Daze?"

Waste deep in the hole, she'd swapped her catsuit for overalls. Standing next to her was Blaze who was wearing identical clothes.

"Hi, Jill." Daze wiped her brow with a muddy hand.

"That looks like hard work."

"It is. And boring."

"I take it you're working undercover?"

"Not exactly. A number of us have been seconded to Z-Branch until the current emergency is over."

"What's Z-Branch?"

"Sorry, I should have explained. Z-Branch is the department in Candlefield that's responsible for monitoring zombie activity in the human world."

"I've never heard it mentioned before, although I am familiar with Z-Watch."

"Z-Watch is an unofficial group of amateurs who play an important part, but Z-Branch is the official body. They're the big guns, if you like."

"Do rogue retrievers often get seconded to them?"

"No, thank goodness. This is my least favourite job, but it is only the second time it's happened since I've been with them, so I shouldn't complain."

"What prompted the call-up this time?"

"We're expecting a major zombie incident tomorrow because it's a full moon."

"I thought the full moon only brought out werewolves. I didn't realise it had an effect on zombies."

"Normally it doesn't, but this is a supermoon."

"A what?"

"It's when the moon appears much larger than normal. For some reason, it brings out the zombies in their hordes."

"Why are you digging the hole?"

"You probably won't be surprised to learn that zombies aren't the smartest of creatures, on account that they have little or no brains. That's quite fortunate really because it makes our job much easier. All we have to do is map their likely routes and then set traps like this one."

"Does that mean you're expecting zombies to come down this road?"

"Yes, but not just this one. There are teams of rogue retrievers digging similar holes throughout this area."

A car horn sounded behind me because the traffic lights were showing green.

"I'd better be going. Good luck with the zombies."

"Thanks, Jill."

***

Jules was at her desk.

"Have you heard about the wedding, Jill? It's so exciting, isn't it?"

"Very." I'd never understood why people got so excited about weddings.

"Did Annabel tell you that she wants you and me to be bridesmaids?"

"Oh, yes."

"I just love the dresses which she's picked out for us. They're beautiful, aren't they?"

"Well — err — "

"Those frills, the giant bow, and I just love pink, don't you?"

"I — err — "

"By the way, did you know that the nail bar has opened?"

"Yeah, they were queuing on the stairs yesterday."

"I hope it's quieter today because I thought I might take advantage of the opening offers, and get my nails done. Why don't you come with me, Jill?" She glanced at my hands. "Your nails could do with some work."

"Thanks, but I think I'll pass."

In all the time I'd known Winky, I'd never seen him look so totally wrecked. He was flat out on the sofa, with one of the kittens sitting on his tummy, and another on his head.

"Help," he managed, weakly.

"Shoo, you two! Get off your uncle!"

The kittens jumped down and scuttled across the room.

"I've barely had a minute's sleep." Winky managed to sit up. "They never stop; they're relentless."

"I thought you had them eating out of your paw?"

"I had no idea that kittens could be such hard work. Will you take them home with you tonight?"

"No chance. You were the one who volunteered for kitten-sitting duties."

"You have to help me, Jill. I can't handle another night like last night. Will you go and get Peggy? She'll know what to do."

"I don't know where she lives."

"I'll give you her address. Please, I'm desperate."

"Okay, I'll do it if I get the time."

Twenty minutes later, I came to the conclusion that there was no point in staying in the office. Have you heard the saying: trying to herd cats? Well, I'd just spent the last fifteen minutes watching *a cat* trying to herd cats (or at least kittens), and he'd failed miserably. The little balls of fur were running Winky ragged, and making me dizzy.

"Don't leave me!" Winky shouted when he saw me headed for the door.

"I'm going to see if I can find Peggy."

"Thank you. I won't forget this."

"Do you think Mrs V will want us to wear pink shoes too?" Jules said.

"I really do hope so."

"Me too."

She obviously didn't have her sarcasm detector switched on.

I'd have to be careful how I played this because I'd got into trouble before when I'd run a similar errand for

Winky.

The man who answered the door seemed friendly enough, although the tattoo of a frog playing the drums, on his neck, was a little distracting.

"I'm sorry to trouble you, but I've found a cat in the building across the way. I'm contacting all the cat owners in the vicinity to see if their cats are missing. The concierge said that you have one?"

"We do, but she's inside, I think." He took a step back. "Lorraine, is Peggy in the flat?"

"Yes, she's asleep on her bed." The woman's voice came from somewhere inside the apartment. "Why?"

"It doesn't matter." He turned back to me. "It's not our cat. Peggy is inside."

"Okay, thanks."

That was part one of my master plan accomplished. At least now, I knew Peggy was inside. For the second part of my plan, I would need the help of magic.

After checking there was no one around, I shrank myself, and then levitated until I was level with the cat flap. Next, I used the 'power' spell to give mini-me the strength to push the flap open. Once inside, I cast the 'invisible' spell, and then searched the apartment until I found Peggy, who was fast asleep on her cat bed. So far, so good, but I would have to be very careful now because the woman of the house was only a few feet away, seated on the sofa, watching a daytime soap.

Invisible mini-me climbed onto the cat bed, and crept along it until I was standing next to the cat's ear.

"Peggy!"

She twitched, but didn't wake up.

"Peggy! Wake up!"

I had to duck as she scratched her ear. And, still she slept on.

"Peggy! Winky needs you."

That seemed to do the trick because she sat up, and looked around, confused.

"It's me, Jill. I'm invisible."

She stared in my direction, but obviously couldn't see me.

"Winky has asked me to come and get you. His niece and nephews have come to stay for a few days, and he can't cope."

Peggy nodded, and then whispered. "I'll get over there now. Will you be okay?"

"Yeah, I'll be fine. You go."

She jumped off the bed, and sprinted for the door. I left at a much more leisurely pace.

***

I didn't head straight back to the office because I wanted to give Peggy time to work her magic. Hopefully, she'd be able to get those little monsters under control.

Before going into Coffee Triangle, I checked to make sure it wasn't drum, gong or triangle day. It turned out to be maracas day, so I treated myself to coffee and a blueberry muffin.

What? It was the least I deserved after my daring foray in search of Peggy.

"You're playing those maracas incorrectly, lady."

The man standing next to my table was wearing jeans and a lumberjack shirt; he had what could only be described as a basin cut.

"Sorry?"

"The maracas. You're not playing them correctly."

"I didn't realise there was a right and wrong way." I gave them another shake.

"No, no. That won't do at all." He snatched them from my hands. "Let me show you. The idea is to get the beads to hit the front of the maracas on the beat. Like this." He demonstrated. "See?"

"I think so."

"Here, try again." He handed them back. "Let the beads roll back, and then strike forward."

"Okay." I tried to follow his instructions. "Like that?"

"Better, but you'll need to keep practising."

"Do you work here?"

"No. I'm from the Washbridge Maracas Society. Our mission is to promote maracas whenever and wherever we can. When we heard about Coffee Triangle, we decided we should pay regular visits on maracas day, to ensure that everyone gets the most out of them. Make sure to keep up the practice."

"I will. Thanks for the tips."

On my way back to the office, as I was walking past Ever, Kathy spotted me through the window, and beckoned me to go inside.

"It's quiet in here," I commented.

"Don't be fooled. I've been run off my feet all day."

"Have you told Grandma that you're—"

"Shush! No, not yet. I don't intend to say anything until I hand in my notice on Friday."

"Are we still on for the seaside tomorrow?"

"Yeah. The coach picks us up on School Lane at eight o'clock. Do you know where that is?"

"It's where Lizzie's school is, isn't it?"

"That's right. Don't be late. Did you and Jack enjoy yourselves last night?"

"Yeah, we did, thanks."

"Only you could buy a foot-spa for someone's anniversary."

"I thought it was an inspired choice. Anyway, you can blame Jack. I told him that he should choose the present."

"Pete likes it. After you two had left, he sat with his feet in it for almost an hour."

"If you two have done chatting on my time." Grandma had crept up behind me. "I'd like a word with you in my office, Jill."

"I'll see you tomorrow morning," I said to Kathy, and then followed Grandma into her lair.

"I hate that woman," Grandma said, once she'd pushed the door to her office closed.

"Hold on! That's my sister you're talking about."

"Not Kathy. I'm talking about Ma Chivers."

"What's she done now?"

"She's been appointed head of the Senior Witches Society."

"The what?"

"It's a bunch of old has-beens who spend all of their time complaining about this or that."

That sounded right up Grandma's street. "Are you a member?"

"Not now. I was for a short while, but I gave up on them. I didn't want to be associated with such a bunch of losers. Somehow, Ma Chivers has wangled her way to the top."

"Why do you care if you have so little regard for the organisation?"

"Because she's using her new platform to spread all manner of malicious rumours about me."

"What kind of rumours?"

"That my powers have diminished. That I've lost my marbles. That kind of thing."

"No one is going to believe her."

"You would think not, but some of the old dears in that organisation are very gullible."

"What are you going to do about it?"

"I'm going to undermine her. Let's see how she likes that."

"Is that all?" I'd expected much worse.

"It will be enough. Just you wait and see."

"Okay, well I suppose I should get going."

"Hold on a minute. Your sister told me that Annabel is going to get married."

"That's right. To Armi."

"How ridiculous. I thought she had more sense."

"What's wrong with them getting married? I think it's lovely."

"If you think it's so lovely, how come you haven't married your human?"

"Jack is not *my human*, and we're not talking about me."

"Do you know where Annabel plans on having her reception?"

"I don't think she's decided yet."

"In that case, you can put a word in for Ever. I plan to hire out the ballroom in between events."

"Will you give her a discount?"

"Good idea. I'll bump up the price, and then knock some off, so she thinks she's getting one."

Unbelievable.

I'd no sooner stepped out of Ever than Betty Longbottom called to me from across the road. At this rate, I'd never make it back to the office.

"Jill, you have to come and see." She beckoned me into the shop.

"I'm rather busy at the moment, Betty. What is it?"

"Come on. You'll be impressed. I promise."

I doubted that, but I had little option but to follow her. To my surprise, she walked all the way through the shop, and out of the rear door.

"Where are we going, Betty?"

"Over there." She pointed to the large building immediately behind the shop.

"Is that where your marine centre is going to be?"

"Eventually yes, but there's a lot of work to do before The Sea's The Limit opens."

Once inside the building, we wound our way down a corridor until we came to a cavernous room.

"Wow!" I looked up at the two huge glass tanks, which were already filled with water.

"These will be the centrepiece of the exhibition," she said.

"How come they're full of water when you've barely started work on the building?"

"We wanted to check they had no leaks before we built around them."

"Is that Sid in there?" I pointed to the scuba diver.

"Yes, he passed the course first time of asking." She

knocked on the glass, and he gave her the thumbs-up. "I can't wait until I qualify so I can join him."

"I'm impressed. The tanks must have set you back a pretty penny."

"We didn't have to spend as much as we'd expected. We managed to find a supplier who came in at less than half what we were originally quoted."

"Really? And the supplier is reputable, I assume?"

"Of course."

When I left Betty, I reflected on how far she'd come since I'd first met her. Back then, she'd been a tax inspector. Now, she was the proud owner of a crustacean gift shop, and would soon be launching a marine centre.

Truly impressive.

Chapter 4

When I eventually made it back to the office, Dexter, Jules' new boyfriend, was standing next to her desk.

"I hope you don't mind me popping in for a few minutes to see Jules?" he said, nervously.

I'd put the fear of god into him the last time I'd seen him. Dexter was a werewolf, and I'd made it clear that if he hurt Jules in any way, he'd have me to answer to.

"Of course not, provided you don't set up camp in here."

"I've been telling Dexter about the wedding," Jules said. "He's looking forward to it, aren't you?"

"Yeah, I love weddings."

Freak!

"That's if we're still together." Jules scowled. "I'm not very happy with him at the moment."

My ears pricked up at that. "Why? What has he done?"

"It's my day off tomorrow; Dexter is off too. I thought we could have a day out together in West Chipping, but misery guts here says he has to work on his car."

"I've already said I'm sorry," Dexter said. "But I really do have to work on it."

"Has it actually broken down?" I asked.

"Well, err—no, but it's—"

"If it hasn't broken down, there's no reason why you couldn't take Jules out tomorrow, and work on the car in the evening, or one day when Jules is working."

"That's just what I said," Jules chimed in.

"I—err—" He obviously felt cornered. "I suppose I could do that."

"Good, that's settled then," I said. "I hope you both

enjoy your day out."

When I went through to my office, the peaceful scene that greeted me was in stark contrast to the one I'd left behind only an hour earlier. The four kittens were sitting in silence, listening to Peggy, telling them a story. Winky was fast asleep on the sofa — no doubt catching up on lost sleep from the previous night. Peggy saw me, and gave me the paws-up.

"I'm reading them a story, and then they're going to have a nap, aren't you kids?"

They all nodded.

And sure enough, twenty minutes later, the four kittens joined Winky in the Land of Nod.

"Well done, Peggy," I said, in a hushed voice.

"There's no need to whisper. This lot will be out for hours. I don't think any of them got much sleep last night."

"Thanks for your help. I really do appreciate it."

"No problem. Anyway, you're not the one who should be thanking me. What was Winky thinking of, agreeing to look after those four?"

"He didn't realise that's what his brother wanted him to do until they all turned up, and by then it was too late. Plus, I reckon he thought that he'd be able to control them."

"He got that part wrong, didn't he?" Peggy rolled her eyes. "I'd better get going."

"Are you leaving?"

"Don't worry. I plan to drop in every few hours to make sure that these four little darlings don't get out of line."

"Thanks. I owe you one."

"No you don't, but sleeping beauty over there definitely does, and I intend to see that he pays his debts. Bye, Jill."

"Bye."

A little later, when Jules came through to my office, cat and kittens were still fast asleep.

"Where did *they* come from?" She did a double-take when she spotted the little balls of fur.

"I'm looking after them for a couple of days for a friend."

"Oh? I'm surprised."

"That I'd look after kittens for someone?"

"No. That you have a friend."

Huh?

Jules continued, "Sorry to bother you, Jill. That Alicia woman is here again. She says it's important."

"You'd better show her through, but no drinks or biscuits for her."

"Oh? Right, okay."

"Thanks for seeing me, Jill."

"What do you want, Alicia?"

"Is it okay if I sit down?"

"I suppose so, but don't get too comfortable."

"Thanks. You have a lot of cats in here."

"You didn't come here to discuss my cats. What's on your mind?"

"I promised that I'd let you know if Ma Chivers was up to anything that might affect you or your family."

"I've already heard that she's been bad-mouthing Grandma, if that's what you're here to tell me."

"She's always done that. No, she's definitely up to something else, but I haven't figured out what it is yet."

"How does that help me then?"

"I think it could be something big, so I figured you'd want to know about it."

"I'm listening."

"She's been running a huge campaign in Candlefield, to recruit witches to work here in Washbridge."

"Doing what?"

"That's just it. No one seems to know. The ads don't give any details, and even the people who have been interviewed for the job, don't seem any wiser. I've spoken to a few of them, and they all said the same thing: that Ma Chivers had been deliberately vague about what the work entailed. The only thing they all agreed on was that the money being offered was good. Good enough that most of the witches I spoke to are tempted to take the offer even though they don't have any idea what they'll be doing."

"She's just opened a wool shop on the high street. Maybe she needs staff for that?"

"Not this many. From what I can make out, she's made job offers to dozens of witches."

"That is weird, and a little scary."

"I just thought you would want to know."

"Right. We'd better exchange phone numbers, in case you find out any more."

After we'd done that, she started for the door.

"Alicia."

"Yeah?"

"Thanks."

***

I wanted to speak to the Bradleys separately, so I'd arranged to meet Georgina at her house, and to meet with Thomas at West Star's offices later in the week.

If I could have picked my dream house (some chance of that on the money that Jack and I made), it would have been something similar to the one owned by the Bradleys. Located in North Wash, a leafy suburb of Washbridge, the house must have been worth at least a million pounds.

"You have a lovely house, Mrs Bradley."

"Thank you. Please call me Georgina. Do come through to the conservatory."

The 'conservatory' was almost as large as the whole of our house, and looked out onto a magnificent rear garden.

"I've made iced tea." She pointed to the glass jug, on the marble-topped table. "Or I can make you something hot if you prefer?"

"Iced tea will be fine, thanks."

After ten minutes of small talk, we got down to business.

"I have to ask about your relationship with Stephen and Thomas, I hope you don't mind?"

"Not at all. I expected you to."

"Your husband said you and he were married five years after Stephen's death?"

"That's right, but Thomas didn't tell you the full story. I think he feels guilty, and I understand why, but if you're going to help us, then I believe it's essential you know everything." She took a deep breath. "Thomas and I were seeing one another before Stephen's death."

"You were having an affair?"

"Yes."

"Did Stephen know about you and his brother?"

"I don't think so. Stephen was very trusting. Too trusting as it turned out. I never wanted to hurt him, but these things sometimes just happen, don't they?"

I was pretty sure that this kind of thing never '*just happened*', but this wasn't the time to voice my opinion, so I waited for her to continue.

"I was the one who wanted to come to you," she said. "Thomas would have preferred to let sleeping dogs lie."

That rather surprised me, but then everything about Georgina Bradley was surprising today. The mouse-like woman who'd visited my office had been replaced by a much more self-assured woman. I wasn't yet sure which one was the 'real' Georgina.

"What motivated you to contact me?"

"This is going to sound crazy."

"Try me."

"I have this niggling doubt that won't go away. I'm afraid that Thomas may have murdered Stephen."

I hadn't seen that one coming.

"Why do you say that?"

"On the night of Stephen's murder, Thomas was supposed to be meeting me, but he called at the last minute to say he would have to work late."

"Was that unusual?"

"His working late wasn't, but cancelling at the last minute like that was. He'd never done it before."

"There must be more to your suspicions than just that?"

"Over recent years, I've seen another side to Thomas. He has a quick temper, and on at least two occasions, I've had to step in to stop him from getting into a fight. It's as though a red mist comes down and he loses control."

"Has he ever been violent towards you?"

"No, but our relationship hasn't been good for over a year now; we argue most of the time."

"Have you ever mentioned your suspicions to the police?"

"No. Back then, it never occurred to me that Thomas might have killed Stephen. He seemed every bit as devastated as I was. And now, I don't feel like I can take this to the police. That's why I wanted to bring you in."

"If Thomas did kill Stephen, why would he agree to come to me?"

"When I first broached the idea, he wasn't very enthusiastic, but he could see how determined I was, so in the end, he agreed."

"It still doesn't make sense. If he is the murderer, he's taking a big risk by allowing me to shine a spotlight on the case again."

"Thomas has never lacked self-confidence. He may think that if he can fool the police, then he can definitely fool you. No offence."

"None taken. Is there anything else that makes you think that he might be the murderer?"

"He and Stephen were at odds over the proposed takeover. Stephen was in favour of taking the money, but Thomas wasn't interested. He wanted to hold onto the business."

"How would it have been resolved if Stephen had lived?"

"It's hard to say. Neither of them had shown any sign of backing down."

"Did Stephen have any enemies? Anyone at all?"

"Not really. Stephen was a gentle, darling of a man."

Which begged the question: why had she cheated on him?

"What exactly are you hoping to get from my investigation?"

"The truth, and justice for Stephen."

"What if it turns out that Thomas isn't the murderer?"

"I'm going to leave him anyway. I've already made my mind up about that, but I don't want to do anything until such time as you've concluded your investigation."

We talked a while longer about both of her husbands, but nothing more of any substance came out of our discussion.

The meeting had not gone the way I'd expected it to. I'd thought I might have to work hard to pry information out of the mouse-like Georgina, but it seemed that she was anything but a mouse. And her accusation that her current husband might have murdered her first husband—his brother—had come completely out of left field. It would be interesting to see how my interview with Thomas Bradley went. Would he be the same man who had visited my office, or would he too be some kind of chameleon?

***

When I got back to the office, there was no sign of Jules, but there was a note on her desk:

Jill, I've gone to Nailed-It. I worked through my lunch hour. Hope this is okay, Jules.

There were no sounds coming from my office, so I opened the door slowly, and tip-toed inside. The kittens were all still flat out, but Winky was wide awake, and sitting on my desk.

"If it isn't Rip Van Winky." I grinned.

"Shush, don't wake the kittens."

"When does Socks get back?"

"Tomorrow, thank goodness. I don't envy him having to look after these little horrors every day."

"Just wait until you and Peggy have your own little ones."

"Don't hold your breath."

"You do realise that you owe Peggy big time for this, I hope?"

"I know. I'll take her for a meal after the kids are off our hands."

While he was speaking, I flicked through the mail, which Jules had dropped onto my desk: Bill, bill, advert, bill. "What's this? It's addressed to the owner of Winky."

"It's obviously for me." He snatched it from my hand.

"It's addressed to your owner."

"I've told you before that I don't have an owner."

He tore open the envelope and studied the letter, which was printed on a pleasing, cream paper. "Very interesting."

"What is it?"

"It's *mind your own business*, that's what it is."

"Have you forgotten that I went to get Peggy for you?"

"Fair enough. It's from Drake, Lake and Makepiece. They're a firm of solicitors. It seems I may have been left something in a Will."

"By who?"

"It doesn't say. My *owner* has to contact them, so you'd better get on the phone to them now."

"But you just said that I'm not your owner."

"Don't try to be smart. Just give them a call to see what it's all about."

"Okay." I called the number on the letter.

"Well? What is it? Have I inherited a fortune?" Winky demanded as soon as I'd finished on the call.

"I don't know."

"What did they say?"

"It's related to the estate of a Mr Shoesmith."

"Never heard of him."

"Apparently, he was your first owner. It seems he bought you as a kitten, but very quickly realised his daughter was allergic to cat fur, so he had to hand you in to a rehoming centre."

"I don't remember that."

"That's not surprising. You were very young. From what they said, you must have been rehomed several times since then because they've had one heck of a job tracing you. Anyway, it seems he's always felt guilty about having to give you up, so he's left you something in his Will."

"Money? How much?"

"We won't know that until the Will is read on Friday."

"I'm going with you. To the reading of the Will."

"I doubt they'll allow a cat in their offices."

"They have to. I'm a beneficiary."

"Okay, but if they turn you away, don't blame me."

"Just think, after Friday, I could be a millionaire."

"What do I get?"

"What do you mean?"

"If I don't turn up for the reading, you won't get a

penny."

"Okay. I'll give you one percent."

I laughed. "Think again. I want half."

"No chance. Ten percent."

"Twenty. Take it or leave it."

"You're a crook."

"It's no skin off my nose whether I go or not."

"Okay. Twenty. I hope you can live with your conscience."

Just then, I heard a strange wailing sound; it was coming from the outer office. My first thought was that one of the kittens had somehow escaped, but the four of them were still sound asleep.

It turned out to be Jules who was in floods of tears at her desk.

"What's wrong?"

"They're ruined."

"What is?"

"My nails. Look!" She held out her hands.

I was no expert on nail care; my own nails are testament to that. But I was quite sure that nails should never have looked like these.

"They are a bit streaky. Is that what you wanted?"

"Of course it isn't. And she's got nail varnish all over my fingers. They look terrible. I can't let Dexter see them. That woman should be arrested."

"Which nail — err — technician did them?"

"There's only one woman working there. I think she's the owner. She's been in here to see you a few times."

"You mean Deli."

"That's her. I thought she was meant to be qualified."

"Now I think about it, I seem to remember she earned her diploma through a correspondence course."

"How can you learn nail care from a correspondence course?"

It was a good question, and one that a lot of her customers would no doubt be asking very soon.

Chapter 5

"Oh, I do like to be beside the seaside."

"Do you have to make that awful row?" Jack looked up from his muesli.

"Don't you like my singing?"

"I wouldn't call that noise singing."

"There's nothing you can say this morning that will upset me because only one person in this room is going to the seaside, and it isn't you."

"It's nice that you don't feel the need to rub it in."

"Oh, I do like to be beside the sea."

"Where are you meeting Kathy?"

"The coach is picking us up near Lizzie's school."

"Do you need me to give you a lift?"

"No, it's okay. I've booked a taxi."

"Any idea what time you'll be home?"

"Late, probably."

"If you give me a call when the coach gets back, I'll come and pick you up unless I'm still at work."

"Thank you, sweetie." I gave him a peck on the lips. "You're so selfless. Just like me."

Half-an-hour later, Jack had left for work, and I was waiting for my taxi to arrive when I felt a vibration in my pocket. At first, I thought it was my phone, but it turned out to be the Z-Call button.

Great! What timing.

Still, great timing or not, I couldn't afford to ignore it, so I called the Z-Watch number.

"Z-Watch. How can I help?"

"Ike? Is that you?"

"Ike Cann speaking."

"It's Jill Gooder. My Z-Call button just vibrated."

"I'll need your passphrase, please."

Oh bum! It was ages since I'd been in touch with Z-Watch, and I couldn't remember my passphrase.

"I can't remember it, but surely the fact that I have the Z-Call button proves it's me?"

"I'm afraid not. Zombies have been known to take the Z-Call button from their victims."

"And what do they do then? Make a phone call? That's hardly likely, is it?"

"There's a first time for everything. Sorry, but I am going to need your passphrase."

"Hold on a minute. It's on the tip of my tongue. Is it 'Custard Creams, the king of biscuits'?"

"No."

"Does it include the word 'Muffin'?"

"I'm afraid I can't give you any clues."

"Wait, hang on. I remember it now: Crazy just got crazier."

"That's it. Nice to hear from you again, Jill. I'm just sorry it had to be under these circumstances."

"What circumstances, exactly?"

"You may not be aware, but there's going to be a Supermoon tonight, which means there's likely to be a lot of zombie activity."

"I did know, actually, because I bumped into some friends of mine who are rogue retrievers. They've been seconded to Z-Branch. When I saw them, they were digging zombie traps."

"And thank goodness for that. The fact that Z-Branch have been deployed illustrates the gravity of the situation.

We're hopeful that the measures they've taken will be enough to ward off a crisis, but we're warning all Z-Watch members to be vigilant tonight, just in case."

"Okay, Ike. Thanks for the heads-up. I'll keep my eyes peeled."

Outside, a car horn sounded; it was my taxi.

"Mornin', darlin'," the cab driver greeted me. "It's nice to pick up someone who doesn't look like a zombie."

"Sorry? Did you say zombie?"

"Most people are still half-asleep when I pick 'em up at this time of day, but you look bright-eyed and bushy-tailed. Are you doing something nice?"

"I'm going to the seaside for the day."

"Want to take me with you?" He laughed. "Ain't got nowt special on."

"Thanks for the offer, but I'm going with my sister."

"Girls' day out, eh? Nice. Where you two going?"

"Frickle-On-Sea."

"I love that place. I used to go there when I was a nipper. You'll be having fish and chips, I'm guessing."

"Probably."

"You have to. It's the law. And candy floss."

When the taxi dropped me off, Kathy was already waiting for me, and to my surprise, Lizzie was standing next to her.

"Morning, you two."

"Hello, Auntie Jill."

"Morning, Jill."

"Won't Lizzie be late for school?"

"I'm not at school today."

"Oh?"

"It's our school trip."

"Right." That made sense. Kathy had obviously decided to take advantage of Lizzie being away for the day. "Where are you going, Lizzie?"

"To the seaside." She turned to Kathy. "What's it called, Mummy?"

"Frickle-On-Sea, darling."

Just then, a crowd of children, accompanied by a few adults, came out of the school gates and began to walk towards us.

Only then, did the penny drop.

"Kathy?" I glared at her.

"Yes?" She gave me her *little miss innocent* look.

Before I could get the words out, a bus came around the corner, parked in front of us, and its doors slid open. By now, the other children had joined us.

"All aboard the Frickle-On-Sea Express," the driver said.

"This is my sister, Jill." Kathy introduced me to the other women.

"It was good of you to volunteer like this." A woman with horn-rimmed glasses shook my hand.

I forced a smile, and then grabbed Kathy by the arm. "Could I have a quick word, please?"

"Sure. Lizzie, you get on the bus and find a seat, while I speak to Auntie Jill."

I wanted to scream at Kathy, but I had to keep it down so that the others wouldn't hear. "This is a school trip!"

"I know."

"I know *you* know, but *I* didn't know."

"I thought I'd mentioned it."

"Liar. This is another of your traps."

"I promised that we'd have a day out at the seaside, and that's what we're getting."

"You, me and a cast of thousands."

"If I hadn't been able to find another responsible adult, the whole trip would have been cancelled."

"*Responsible*? Me? I'm the most irresponsible person I know."

"You're not going to let Lizzie down now, are you?"

"Of course I'm not. You knew I'd have to go along with it once I was here."

"Come on. We'd better get on board; they're waiting for us."

"I'll get you back for this."

The woman with the horn-rimmed glasses turned out to be Mrs Plum, the headmistress. When we were halfway to Frickle-On-Sea, she swapped seats with Kathy for a few minutes, so she could speak to me.

"Thank you again for helping us out at such short notice, Jill."

"No problem," I said, through gritted teeth.

"Kathy told me how excited you were to be involved."

"Did she now?"

"I gather you and your sister are very close."

"Oh yes, very." But probably not after today.

"We have quite a full day planned."

"Lots of sunbathing on the beach, I assume."

"Definitely not. It wouldn't do for us to waste all day on the beach, would it?"

"Wouldn't it? No, I suppose not."

"Here." She handed me a sheet of paper. "This is the

schedule for the day."

"The Frickle-On-Sea Museum?"

"I thought it best to go there first because it will probably get busy later."

"Really?" Who cares about some boring museum? Yawn. "The Fishing Net Craft Centre? What's that?"

"Frickle-On-Sea used to be a major fishing port. Although that's no longer the case, the craft centre gives demonstrations on how the fishing nets used to be made. I've seen it a couple of times, and I have to say it's fascinating."

"I bet."

"Sorry?"

"I bet it's really interesting." More yawns.

"It certainly is."

"Then lunch?" I said. "I assume we'll be getting fish and chips?"

"Certainly not. All that fat? The children were told to bring sandwiches. Didn't Kathy tell you to bring something?"

"She must have forgotten."

"Not to worry. You're welcome to share mine. I have egg and cress sandwiches."

"Yummy."

The headmistress went on to talk me through the afternoon's activities, but I was practically comatose by then.

"What about the beach?" I asked. "Surely, the kids will want to play on the sand?"

"Of course. Look." She pointed to the last item on her 'schedule'. "I've allocated thirty minutes before we get back on the coach."

Thirty whole minutes? Whoopee!

"You and Mrs Plum seemed to hit it off," Kathy said, after she'd swapped seats with the headmistress again.

"Have you seen her 'schedule' for the day?"

"Yeah. There's an awful lot to cram in."

"And it's all boring stuff. It's the kids I feel sorry for. I'm sure they'd prefer to build sandcastles, and paddle in the sea, instead of listening to someone drone on about the history of fishing nets."

"It could be interesting."

"How did you manage to say that with a straight face?"

"Don't you remember when we had that school trip to the cotton mill museum?"

"No."

"You must do. We saw lots of cotton-spinning machinery."

"It was probably so boring that I've erased it from my memory."

"You always were shallow, Jill."

Okay, I admit it. The Frickle-On-Sea Museum was actually quite interesting. It was weird to look back at old photographs taken at the resort; some of them dated back to the early part of the previous century. I could definitely picture Grandma wearing the type of bathing costumes they wore back then.

The Fishing Net Craft Centre was a different matter. It turned out to be every bit as boring as I'd expected. To be fair, most of the kids seemed to find it enjoyable. They were all given an opportunity to make a small section of fishing net.

Not only was I bored, but I was starving too, and the only thing I had to look forward to was a few egg and cress sandwiches.

"Having fun?" Kathy had come over to join me.

"Oh yeah, it's a laugh a minute. Can you watch the kids while I nip to the loo?"

"Sure. No problem."

I hurried back to the front of the building. Everyone had been told to leave their sandwich boxes in a cupboard, close to the main entrance doors. After checking there was no one around, I sneaked inside, cast the 'hide' spell, and then went back to join Kathy and the kids.

"Okay, children," the headmistress said. "It's time for lunch now. We'll collect our sandwich boxes, and go and sit in the park."

Everyone followed her to the cupboard.

"They've gone!" She gasped.

"They can't have." Kathy checked for herself. "Who would steal a load of sandwich boxes?"

"I'm starving, Miss!" A young boy shouted.

"Me too!" The little girl next to him looked tearful.

Soon, all the kids had joined in.

"There's a fish and chip shop just across the road," I shouted over the din. "Why don't we go there?"

"I—err—don't think—" the headmistress began, but her objections were drowned out by the kids who were all very keen. In the end, she relented, "Okay, I suppose we have no choice under the circumstances."

The fish, chips and mushy peas were to die for.

Kathy came to join me. "These are delicious."

"They're definitely better than egg and cress sandwiches."

"What do you think could have happened to the sandwich boxes?"

"Who knows? People will steal anything these days."

Straight after lunch, we were forced to endure a walking tour of the old port. That left only two items on the infamous 'schedule'. Next was a two-hour tour of the botanical gardens, followed by thirty minutes on the beach, and then home.

Don't get me wrong, I enjoy a few flowers as much as the next person, but I had no desire to spend two hours looking at them, and I was sure that the kids didn't. It was time for me to step in again.

"Kathy. Watch the kids while I go to the loo, would you?"

"Again?"

"Sorry. I won't be long."

I didn't have much time, so I cast the 'faster' spell to get me to the botanical gardens in a matter of seconds. Once there, I quickly cast the spell that I was relying on to rescue what was left of our day, and then I rushed back to the kids.

Fifteen minutes later, we all arrived at the gates of the botanical gardens — only to find them locked.

"Sorry." A man wearing a blue uniform and cap was standing in front of the gates. "You can't come in, I'm afraid."

"Why not?" Mrs Plum sounded indignant. "We've travelled a long way to get here today."

"I'm sorry, madam, but I'm sure you wouldn't want your little darlings to become the lion's next meal."

"*Lion?*"

"Yes. There's a lion loose inside."

"Where did it come from?"

"That's a very good question. No one seems to know."

"Is there a zoo around here?"

"No zoo. No circus. It's something of a mystery."

The headmistress turned to face us. "I'm very sorry, children. I know you'll be disappointed to hear that we can't go into the botanical gardens."

"Why don't we spend more time on the beach?" I suggested. "Kids? Would you like that?"

The chorus of 'yesses' was deafening.

"Err—I—err—suppose that would be okay," Mrs Plum agreed reluctantly.

And so it was that we got to spend the next two-and-a-bit hours on the beach. Sandcastles were built (and destroyed), the kids paddled, and much fun was had. The adults hired deckchairs, and spent an enjoyable afternoon doing very little.

"This is more like it." I sighed.

"I don't understand where the lion could have come from," Kathy said.

"It's a mystery for sure, but I reckon it turned out for the best. The kids have enjoyed the beach much more than they would have the botanical gardens."

On the way home, most of the kids dozed on the coach. They were exhausted from running up and down the beach.

"Today wasn't so bad after all, was it?" Kathy said.

"The fish and chips and the beach made it bearable."

"Am I forgiven, then?"

"Definitely not. You don't get off that easily."

"I still can't understand how the sandwich boxes turned up on the coach."

"That was a little weird."

"Not as weird as the lion, though." Kathy was staring at her phone. "According to my news app, the lion disappeared into thin air."

Jack had to work late, but Peter was on hand to drop me at the house. It was almost eleven o'clock when Jack eventually got back home.

"Hello, sexy." He greeted me with a kiss and a cuddle. "Did you and Kathy have a good day at the seaside?"

"Yes, it was fantastic."

"Really?" He smirked. "What about all the kids? Did they enjoy it?"

"How did you know about the kids?"

"Peter told me."

"Hang on. *When* did he tell you?"

"This morning before you came downstairs. Kathy asked him to call to make sure you were up."

"You knew it was a school trip, and you didn't tell me?"

"I was going to, but then you started to gloat because I had to go to work while you were having a day at the seaside."

"I did not gloat."

"Not much. Now, what was it you were singing? Oh yes, I remember. Oh, I do like to be beside the seaside."

"I hate you."

"Come on, Jill, you have to see the funny side."

"Which is?"

"That you thought you were getting a girls' day out, but instead you became a school teacher for the day."

"I'm going to bed." I started for the door.

"Did you remember to buy me a stick of rock?"

"I did, and you know where you can shove it, don't you?"

Chapter 6

By the next morning, I'd decided to be magnanimous and forgive Jack for the previous day.

What do you mean I'd been in the wrong too? Don't be ridiculous.

I was in the kitchen, munching my way through two slices of toast; Jack had popped out to get a newspaper.

"The Bugle has really surpassed itself this time," he said when he walked back in. "What a headline."

"I thought you only wanted the newspaper for the ten-pin bowling scores?"

"I do, but just listen to this headline: Zombies spotted in Washbridge."

"What? Are there photos?"

"Of course there aren't photos." He looked at me as though I'd just fallen out of the stupid tree, and hit every branch on the way down. "You do realise that zombies aren't real, don't you?"

"Err—yeah, of course. What does it say?"

"Just that the newspaper has received several calls from people in different areas of Washbridge who all claim to have seen a zombie."

"That's weird."

"You know why this has happened, don't you? It's because of the full moon. People go crazy and imagine all kinds of stuff when there's a full moon."

"That must be it. I—err—I'd better put out the trash."

"I've already done it."

"Right. I'll go and check on the sandpit, then."

"What's to check? It was still there ten minutes ago."

"I want to make sure the local cats haven't been using it

as a litter tray." I grabbed my coat and hurried outside.

When I'd arrived home from the seaside the previous day, I'd totally forgotten that I was supposed to be keeping a watch out for zombies. I needed to check in with Z-Watch to get an update.

"Z-Watch. How can I help?"

"Is that Ike?"

"Ike's not here at the moment. This is Noel Knowles."

"Noel—?"

"Knowles, yes. How can I help?"

"It's Jill Gooder. I'm a member of Z-Watch. I just wanted to check how things went last night."

"Catchphrase please?"

"Crazy just got crazier."

"Hi, Jill. It's been one heck of a night as you can imagine."

"I've just seen the headlines in The Bugle."

"The traps set by Z-Branch caught most of the undead, but a few stragglers got through."

"There doesn't appear to be any photos, thank goodness."

"That's because Z-Branch had the foresight to bring over some specially trained witches and wizards who were tasked with intercepting any humans who caught sight of the zombies. They used magic to make the humans forget, and then manually erased any photos they may have taken. Fortunately, it appears that the few humans they missed hadn't taken photos. We were very lucky this time."

"Do we have an all-clear now?"

"We're asking members to continue to be vigilant because there's every chance that there may still be a few zombies around. Hopefully, they'll all be mopped up by the end of the morning."

"Okay, Noel. Thanks very much for the update."

***

"Who were you on the phone to?" Jack asked when I went back inside. He must have seen me through the back window.

"It was Mrs V. Apparently, she's decided on white limousines for the wedding."

"She rang you at this time of the morning to tell you that?"

"I told you how excited she was about the wedding."

"I can't blame her. I'm looking forward to it, too."

"That makes one of us."

"I'm especially looking forward to seeing you in your sexy bridesmaid's outfit."

"Can we not discuss bridesmaid's dresses at this time in the morning? Just thinking about it gives me heartburn."

***

When I left for work, I noticed that one of the back doors of Megan's van was open. I couldn't see the woman herself, so thought I'd better make sure no one was helping themselves to her gardening tools.

As I got closer, I could hear noises coming from inside the van, and assumed it must be Megan.

"Morning, Meg—" I froze.

The occupant of the van wasn't Megan, unless she'd really let herself go since the last time I'd seen her. The zombie had somehow climbed inside, but didn't have enough brain (if indeed he had any) to get out again. He was walking back and forth, crashing into the sides of the van.

"Morning, Jill." Megan suddenly appeared in her doorway.

"Hi." I quickly pushed the van door closed.

"Thank goodness." She came around the van to join me. "When I got up this morning, I had a horrible feeling that I'd left one of the van doors open last night."

"Nope. They're both shut."

"You must think I'm ditzy. It's just that I had such a hectic day yesterday that by the time I got home, I was out on my feet."

"I have days like that too."

Just then, the zombie thudded against the wall of the van, so to distract Megan, I quickly thumped the side. "These are excellent vans. I wouldn't mind getting one."

"Really? What would you use it for in your line of business?"

"I—err—I could use it for undercover surveillance."

"Of course. Well, I'd better get going. I have an early appointment."

"Wait!" I screamed at her.

"What's wrong?"

"I—err—just wondered if you could give me a lift. My car won't start."

"I'd be happy to, but I'm not actually going into Washbridge. My appointment is in Middle Wash."

"That's lucky. I have to meet with a client in Middle Wash this morning."

"You do? Right, well climb in."

"Do you mind if we have the radio on?" I didn't wait for an answer; I just turned the volume to 'max'. My eardrums were on the point of bleeding, but at least we couldn't hear the zombie.

We were halfway to Middle Wash when Megan pulled into a layby.

"I'm sorry, Jill." She turned down the volume. "I don't know how you can stand it that loud. It's giving me earache."

"Sorry. I wasn't—"

Just then, there was a thud in the back of the van, followed by another.

"There's someone in the back." Megan was out of the door before I could stop her.

I jumped out and rushed around the back to find her about to open the door.

"Stop!"

I cast the 'sleep' spell, and caught her before she slumped to the floor. After casting the 'power' spell, I carried her back to the driver's seat. Once she was settled, I made my way to the back of the van, threw open the door, and fired a 'thunderbolt' which blew the zombie to smithereens.

Once I was back in the cab, I reversed the 'sleep' spell, and Megan woke up.

"You're right," I said.

"Sorry?"

"The music was too loud. I'm sorry. I wasn't thinking."

"Right, yeah. Okay." Still a little confused, she drove on to Middle Wash.

"Where do you want me to drop you, Jill?" she asked when we arrived in the village.

"Anywhere here will be fine."

"How will you get back after you've finished your interview?"

"Don't worry. I'll get a taxi."

"I'd offer to take you home, but I'm going to be working here most of the day."

"No problem. Thanks again for the lift."

Once she'd driven off, and I'd made sure there was no one else around, I magicked myself back to the house.

Zombies: Nil.

Jill Gooder: One.

***

Mr Ivers was in the toll booth, but he didn't even look up when I pulled up. I was just about to call to him when a mechanical arm swung out.

"Drop the cash onto the hand please, Jill," Mr Ivers said.

I did as he asked, and the arm swung slowly back inside.

"That's quite ingenious," I said.

"Thank you. I had to come up with something for the sake of my elbows. My cousin is an engineer; he was the one who made it. I call it Andy." He laughed. "Get it?"

"That's—err—almost funny."

***

Jules was at her desk. Her eyes were red, and she'd obviously been crying.

"What's wrong?"

"It's nothing, Jill."

"Come on. There's obviously something the matter."

"It's Dexter."

"What's he done?" If that werewolf had hurt her, I'd kill him.

"He left me."

"Do you mean he's dumped you?"

"No, well—err—I don't know. Maybe. He left me behind in West Chipping, yesterday."

"I'll make a cup of tea, and you can tell me all about it."

"Everything was okay at first. I thought we were having a lovely day. We went to the park, and then we had a delicious meal in the pub near to the duck pond. I was just thinking how much nicer Dexter was than Gilbert, when he jumped up, rushed to his car, and drove away."

"What did he say?"

"He didn't say anything. He just drove off."

"Had you been arguing?"

"No. One minute we were chatting, and the next he'd gone."

"What did you do? How did you get home?"

"I had to call a taxi."

"Have you tried to get in touch with him since?"

"I've phoned and texted, but he hasn't replied. I don't know what I did wrong."

"You didn't do anything wrong. Where does he work?"

"Why?"

"I just wondered."

"At the exhaust centre near to the library."

"Right. Will you be okay to work today?"

"Yeah, I'm fine. I need something to take my mind off what happened."

"Okay. I'll check on you later to make sure you're alright."

"Thanks, Jill."

I was relieved to find that the cat count in my office was back to just the one.

"I see Socks has taken the kids back. I bet you're glad to see the back of those little monsters?"

"Not at all. I'm missing them already. They were a lot of fun."

"You were ready for drowning them before Peggy came to your rescue."

"Okay, I admit Peggy did help a little." He gestured to the outer office. "The pretty young thing has been crying since she got here. What's up with her?"

"It's that new boyfriend of hers."

"What's he done?"

"I'm not sure, but I intend to find out."

"You haven't forgotten that you're taking me to the solicitors tomorrow, have you?"

"Of course not, but I wouldn't go building up your hopes. It may amount to nothing."

"I have a good feeling about this. Why would he go to all the trouble of tracing me unless he was going to leave me a substantial amount? I was looking at watches online earlier. You can get some really nice ones for less than ten grand."

"You know what they say about chickens, don't you?"

"That they love to cross the road whilst being mysterious about their motives?"

Halfway through the morning, Jules came through to

my office. At first, I thought she was still upset, but then I realised her expression was one of anger.

"It's that woman."

"Sorry, Jules, you're going to have to give me a little more than that."

"The Nailed-It woman. She's out there with a man. I don't know how she dare show her face."

I glanced at Jules' hands. "I see you managed to salvage your nails."

"It took me ages, and they still aren't as good as they were before I went to her stupid nail bar. Do you think I could sue her, Jill?"

"I don't think it would be worth your while. Deli isn't exactly rolling in money. Would you show them in, please?"

I'd never seen Deli like this. Usually, she was larger than life, and the life and soul of the party, but today, she looked defeated. Nails had to help her into the office.

"Deli? Are you okay?"

"It's all gone wrong, Jill." She slumped into the chair. Nails stood behind her with his hands on her shoulders.

"What has?"

"The nail bar. Everyone is complaining. They're all saying I've ruined their nails."

"What went wrong? I thought you'd done a course?"

"I did, but I've never actually had to work on a real person before. The correspondence course provided us with artificial hands to practise on. The real things are much more difficult. I don't know what to do, Jill."

Before I could say anything, Nails chipped in, "I've told her that she should let me take over."

"You?" I couldn't hide my surprise at his suggestion.

"I've always done Deli's nails for her, haven't I, lover?"

She nodded.

"Show Jill your nails," he said.

She held out her hands, and although I was no expert, her nails did look a million times better than Jules' had after her trip to Nailed-It.

"It's supposed to be my business," Deli said.

"It still will be, lover. I'll just hold the fort until you've had time to get up to speed on real hands."

"Who will I practise on?"

"You can practise on me, in the evenings," he said.

I was really touched by this show of affection from the usually undemonstrative Nails.

"What do you think I should do, Jill?" Deli said.

"I don't see you have any choice but to let Nails give it a go. Things can't be any worse, can they?"

"I suppose you're right." She took a moment to compose herself. "Okay, enough of feeling sorry for myself. Let's do this." She stood up. "Thanks, Jill."

"I didn't really do anything."

"You're a good listener. Mad always said you were. Come on, Nails, your next appointment is in ten minutes."

***

When I pulled into the exhaust centre, I was greeted by a grease monkey who had a cigarette butt stuck behind his ear. "Looks like it's a new car you need, love, not an exhaust."

"I'm not here for either, and I'll thank you to keep your comments to yourself."

"It was only a joke, Mrs. No need to get your knickers in a knot."

"Where can I find Dexter?"

"Are you his new bird? He never mentioned he'd found himself an older woman."

"Shut it or I'll shove that spanner where the sun doesn't shine."

"I like a bird with a bit of spark." He grinned. "Dexter's over there on his break."

Dexter was the only person in the small staff room. When he saw me, he stood up and backed into a corner. He looked like a rabbit caught in the headlights.

"Jill? What are you doing here? Is Jules okay?"

"What do you think? Some lowlife left her stranded in West Chipping yesterday."

"I can explain."

"This should be good."

"It's actually all your fault."

"Wow! You've really got some nerve."

"It's true. I'd done my best to get out of taking her out yesterday, but then you more or less forced me into it."

"What's that got to do with the price of fish?"

"It was the full moon yesterday."

My heart sank as I realised what I'd done.

He continued, "I hoped I'd be able to get her back home in time for me to go to the Range in Candlefield, but she was enjoying herself so much that she wanted to stay. I waited as long as I dared, but then I had to make a run for it. If I'd stayed any longer, I'd have turned. I dread to think what might have happened then."

"It's my fault, Dexter. I should have realised what you

were doing when you said you had to work on your car. I'm sorry."

"How is Jules?"

"Not great, as you can imagine."

"She's tried to contact me, but I don't know what to say to her."

"Don't worry about it. This is my mess, so I'll sort it out. You'd better give me your phone number, so I can let you know how I get on."

Chapter 7

I headed straight back to the office where Jules still looked down in the dumps.

"I've just been to see Dexter," I said.

"Why?"

"I had intended to give him a piece of my mind, but it seems that he had a very good reason for leaving you in the lurch like that."

"Really? What?"

"When you were in West Chipping, he received a text to say his grandmother had been taken seriously ill. For a while, it was touch and go if she'd make it or not."

"Why didn't he say anything?"

"His mind was in a whirl. All he could think of was that he needed to get to his grandmother's bedside before—err—in case—you know."

"Poor Dexter. And I said all those awful things about him. How is his grandmother? She's not—?" Her voice trailed away.

"No, she pulled through, but she's still in hospital. That's why he hasn't got around to answering your calls or messages."

"Do you think I should try to call him again now?"

"It would probably be better to wait until he contacts you. I'm sure you'll hear from him soon."

"Okay. Thanks for doing this, Jill."

"No problem."

Once I was in my office, I made a call to Dexter.

"I don't have a grandmother," he said. "They both died when I was a toddler."

"It's too late to change the story now. It shouldn't matter, anyway. Jules will just be pleased to hear from you, but I would wait until later today or tomorrow. Just make sure you stick to the story: your grandmother took very ill, but is a little better now."

"I don't like the idea of lying to her, Jill."

"Do you have a better idea? You can hardly tell her the truth, can you?"

"I suppose you're right. Thanks for your help."

"It's the least I can do. I was the one who got you into this mess."

"What was that all about?" Winky asked, after I'd finished on the call.

"I'm trying to help sort out Jules' love life, but it means her boyfriend, Dexter, will have to tell a little white lie. I can understand him not being very happy about doing that because I hate having to tell lies too."

Winky burst out laughing.

"What's so funny?"

"You're a compulsive liar. You lie even when you don't need to."

"That's rubbish. I don't remember the last time I told a lie."

"There! Right there. That's another one."

***

The West Star advertising agency occupied the top floor of the Nexler Building. The receptionist directed me to the large office suite at the far end of that floor. Inside the suite, a smartly dressed woman greeted me.

"You must be Jill Gooder." The woman came out from behind her desk. "I'm Ruth Foot, Thomas's PA." She offered her hand. She was wearing what was probably the ugliest ring I'd ever seen. It took me a few moments to work out what it was, but then I realised it was shaped like a small foot.

"Nice to meet you, Ruth."

"It was a present from my mother."

"Sorry?"

"I saw you looking at my ring. My mother gave it to me a few months before she died."

"It's very — err — unusual."

"A one-off. She had it specially made. It's a foot. Like my name."

"Right. Is Thomas around?"

"He's up on the roof. He has a cigarette break every hour on the hour. Can I get you something to drink while you wait?"

"No, thanks. I'm okay. Have you worked here long, Ruth?"

"Since the very beginning. When we first moved in, the suite you're now standing in was the whole of West Star. Back then, I was PA and general dogsbody to both Thomas and Stephen."

Before I could ask any more questions, the door behind me opened, and in walked Thomas Bradley.

"I'm sorry to have kept you waiting."

"No problem."

"Ruth will no doubt have told you about my disgusting smoking habit."

"I'm surprised you're allowed to smoke up there."

"Officially, we're not, but it's such a long way down to

the street. The owners of the building send around a memo every few months, reminding us of the smoking ban, but I ignore it. Anyway, would you care for a drink?"

"Ruth has already asked me, thanks. I'm fine."

"In that case, why don't you come through to my office?"

"This is very impressive." I glanced around. "It puts mine to shame."

"It wasn't always like this. When we first moved in, this room was actually two offices: one was mine, the other was Stephen's."

"Ruth tells me she's been with you from the start?"

"That's right. How she's managed to put up with me for so long, I'll never know."

"Is it okay if we get straight down to business?"

"Of course. I'm all yours."

"I'm curious to know whose idea it was to come to me after all of this time?"

"It was mine. Georgina wasn't very enthusiastic. She didn't think there was anything you could do that the police haven't already done."

"When you came to my office, you said that you and Georgina had become close after Stephen's death."

"That's right."

"When I spoke to Georgina by herself, she told me that you and she were having an affair before Stephen was murdered."

"She told you that?"

"Why didn't you mention it before?"

"I thought I was protecting her. I'm very surprised she told you."

"She doesn't think that Stephen knew about the affair."

"He didn't. Definitely not. We were very discreet."

"In my job, I come across a lot of couples who think they're being discreet, but there are usually clues if you know where to look for them. Isn't it possible that Stephen knew about your affair?"

"No. He would have confronted me."

"Is that what happened? Did he confront you on that night?"

"No. I've just told you he had no idea about the affair. What exactly are you suggesting?"

"I'm not suggesting anything; I'm just looking for answers. I understand that you worked late the night that Stephen died?"

"That's right."

"Georgina said that you'd originally planned to meet her that night, but then cried off."

"That's true. Something urgent cropped up at the last minute, but I still got away before Stephen. He was fine when I left. You surely don't think I had anything to do with his death? Would I have come to see you if I had?"

"If I'm going to find the murderer, it's essential you tell me the whole truth. The fact that you omitted to tell me about the affair makes me wonder if there's anything else you're holding back."

"There's nothing else, I promise. I'm sorry I didn't mention the affair, but as I said, I thought I was protecting Georgina. I can see now that wasn't necessary."

"Would you say that you and Georgina have a happy marriage?"

"What kind of question is that? Of course we do. We've never been happier. I really fail to see what any of this has to do with Stephen's death."

"Why don't we talk about the proposed takeover?"

"What do you want to know?"

"Who was trying to take over West Star?"

"Mondale. They were one of the big players at the time, but they went bust about three years after Stephen died."

"Why were you against the takeover? The money must have been tempting?"

"Money isn't everything. West Star was only small back then, but we'd already attracted a number of blue-chip clients. And besides, Stephen was deluding himself. He thought he'd be able to take the money and walk away. There was no way that Mondale would have let either of us do that. They didn't really want to buy the business; they wanted to buy the two of us because, essentially, we were West Star. They would have tied us to the business for at least seven years. I was used to being my own boss, and I had no desire to give that up."

"Stephen must have been angry that you blocked the takeover?"

"He was, but he would have got over it eventually."

"I'd like to talk about the night of Stephen's murder."

"Okay."

"Who was in the office?"

"Just Stephen and I."

"What about Ruth?"

"From memory, she stayed until about eight, but then went home. Stephen was working in his office; I was in mine."

"Did either of you have any visitors during that time?"

"I didn't. I don't think Stephen did."

"Aren't you sure?"

"No. Back then, the offices weren't like this." He gestured to the glass walls. "The only windows were those in the doors. We couldn't see into each other's office."

"Wouldn't you have heard voices if he'd had any visitors?"

"Probably, and I didn't."

"What time did you leave?"

"Sometime between ten and ten-thirty."

"And you're sure Stephen was okay then?"

"Positive. I popped into his office to tell him I was leaving."

"What happened the next day?"

"When I arrived, the police were already here. Ruth had found Stephen dead in his office."

"I asked Georgina if Stephen had any enemies; she said that he didn't. Is that true?"

"Yes, I would say so. The advertising game is a tough one, and we had competitors who wouldn't have been sorry to see us go out of business, but there was no one who would wish Stephen dead."

"Who do *you* think killed Stephen?"

"I honestly don't know."

It had proved to be an interesting meeting. Although it had yielded no clues as to who murdered Stephen Bradley, it had exposed discrepancies between the stories told by Thomas and Georgina. She'd said it was her idea for them to come to me, but he'd insisted it was his. He'd maintained the reason for not telling me about the affair was to protect Georgina, and yet she'd been only too happy to tell me about it. Georgina had said that their relationship was in trouble, and that she intended to leave Thomas, but he insisted they were as happy as they'd ever been.

They couldn't both be telling the truth.

***

I was on my way back to the office when my phone rang.

"Jill, it's Dexter." He sounded panic-stricken.

"What's wrong?"

"I rang Jules a couple of minutes ago."

"Already? I told you to wait a while."

"I'm sorry. I just wanted to make sure we were okay."

"What did she say?"

"She was really lovely about it all."

"So what's wrong?"

"She wants to visit my grandmother in hospital with me."

"Please tell me you said that wouldn't be possible."

"She caught me off-guard."

"What did you say?"

"That she could."

"You idiot."

"I'm sorry."

"You have to call her back and tell her she can't go."

"If I do that now, she'll think I've been making it all up. You have to help me, Jill. You were the one who came up with the idea of my grandmother."

"When are you supposed to be taking her?"

"Tonight."

"Okay, try not to panic."

"It's too late for that. I'm losing my mind here."

"Everything's going to be alright."

"How?"

"I'll think of something. What time have you arranged to pick up Jules?"

"Seven o'clock."

"Right. Go ahead and do that."

"Then what?"

"I don't know yet, but I'll send you a text as soon as I do."

I ended the call before he had the chance to ask more questions that I couldn't answer. How on earth had I managed to get myself into such a mess?

What? Alright, I know. It's my own fault for lying. Are you happy now? Sheesh!

I'd no sooner finished on the call to Dexter than my phone rang again.

"Aunt Lucy?"

"Jill, our offer for the new house has been accepted."

"That's great. I'm really happy for you."

"Are you alright, Jill? You sound a bit stressed."

"I am a little. I'm okay, though."

"I'm just going over to the new house. Why don't you come with me? It'll take your mind off things."

"Yeah, I think I will. I'll be with you in a minute."

Aunt Lucy was waiting for me outside her house.

"We'll take the car, Jill. You can drive."

"Okay."

I'd never seen Aunt Lucy quite so excited; she talked non-stop during the short journey over to her new house.

"Which one is it?" I asked when we pulled up outside a pair of semi-detached cottages, both of which had a 'For Sale' sign in their garden.

"The one on the left. They're owned by two elderly sisters who have decided to move to the seaside."

"They look identical."

"They are, pretty much. We had a difficult time deciding which one to make an offer on. In the end, we went for this one because the rear garden is slightly larger. Come and take a look inside."

"Are they leaving any of the furniture?"

"Matilda, that's the sister who's selling this house, has said we can buy any of the furniture in the lounge or bedrooms if we want to. She and her sister will be sharing a house after they move, so they won't need to take it all with them."

"The sofa and chairs look practically new. And the sideboard is gorgeous."

"I agree. Lester and I have decided to buy those, and a wardrobe too. At the prices she's asking, we'd be fools not to."

The rest of the cottage did not disappoint. Although it was smaller than Aunt Lucy's current house, it had way more character, and was certainly big enough for just her and Lester.

After she'd shown me all around the house, Aunt Lucy took me out into the rear garden.

"This needs some work," I said.

"Matilda and her sister have found it difficult to keep on top of their gardens. Still, that's not a problem; Lester and I will soon knock this into shape. And if we need any help, we can always call on you."

"Me?"

"It's okay. I'm only joking. We're actually looking forward to the challenge."

"Have you told Grandma that you're moving, yet?"

"No, but I'll have to soon because the 'For Sale' sign will be going up at our house."

"I'm sure she'll be thrilled for you." I grinned.

"Somehow, I doubt that." Aunt Lucy checked her watch. "I'd better get back, so I can get started on dinner."

"Will you drive, Aunt Lucy? I'd like you to drop me at Cuppy C on the way past if you don't mind. I could kill for a muffin."

"No problem. By the way, you haven't forgotten that you promised to check out that modelling agency for Barry, have you?"

"To be honest, it had completely slipped my mind."

"It hasn't slipped his. He keeps asking if I've heard from you. What shall I tell him?"

"Tell him that I'm going to check it out today, would you? I'll go there as soon as I've had a coffee and muffin."

***

Pearl was behind the counter in the tea room, but there was no sign of Amber.

"My usual, please."

"Five blueberry muffins?"

"Very funny. Just one will do. Where's Amber?"

"Shopping with William. She's taking liberties; this is the second time I've been stuck here by myself this week."

"I saw her after she'd been for a check-up. What about

you? Have you had yours yet?"

"Yeah. Everything's fine." Pearl passed me the coffee and muffin. "I'm glad I've caught you by yourself because—"

"Excuse me, love." A young man wearing a grey uniform appeared at my side. "I'm here about the smart meter."

The man's uniform looked several sizes too big for him, and with the cap pulled down over his eyes, I could barely see his face. He was really struggling to carry the large toolbox he had with him.

"It's through here." Pearl beckoned him to follow her.

"Weird guy," I said when she returned.

"Takes all sorts. They're replacing the old meters with smart ones. Hopefully, the new one will save us a bit of money."

"You were about to tell me something."

"Was I? Oh yeah, I remember. Alan and I have come up with names for the baby. Would you like to hear them?"

"Of course."

"If it's a girl, we're going to call her Lily. Lil for short. And if it's a boy, we'll call him—"

"Phil?"

"No. Bill. They rhyme, did you notice?"

"So they do. Have you and Amber discussed names?"

"No. I know what she's like. She'll nick our ideas. You won't tell her, will you, Jill?"

"Of course not. My lips are sealed."

Chapter 8

The Pooch First Model Agency was only a stone's throw from Cuppy C. Their offices were located on a side street, above a fishmonger. The vampire who had given the business card to Aunt Lucy had said I should phone, but I thought I'd get a better feel for the operation if I could see their offices, and speak to someone face-to-face. I'd heard lots of horror stories about modelling agencies who made a living not by finding their clients work, but by charging for things such as providing photos for a portfolio. Granted, those had been agencies for humans rather than for animals, but if anything, I was even more suspicious of an agency which represented only dogs.

The name of the business was embossed on the frosted glass in the door. I knocked, but there was no reply, so I tried the door and found it was unlocked.

The room was small, but tastefully decorated. The desk looked antique, and not too dissimilar to my own.

"Hello? Anyone home?"

"I'll be with you in a minute." The man's voice came from behind a second door at the back of the room.

While I waited, I looked around the office. Framed photographs of dogs of all shapes and sizes adorned every wall. In between two of the photos was a framed certificate that confirmed Scott Basset was a member of the Canine Modelling Association.

"Sorry to keep you waiting." The man was smartly dressed in what looked like a Harris Tweed suit. "I've been meaning to have a clear out back there for months."

"Are you Mr Basset?"

"I am, but please call me Scott. How can I help you?"

"You gave your business card to my dog. Or at least to my aunt who was walking him in the park."

"You're Barry's owner?"

"That's right." I was surprised and more than a little impressed that he knew which dog I was referring to. Until then, I'd assumed he handed out his business card willy-nilly. "How did you know?"

"You mentioned the park. I've only come across one dog that was of interest to me in there recently. A very handsome labradoodle he is too."

"Thank you. Barry said that you wanted me to phone, but I thought it would be better for me to speak to you in person. I hope you don't mind my calling in without an appointment?"

"Not at all, and especially not if your visit means that you're interested in allowing Barry to sign with us."

"Let's not get ahead of ourselves. I'll be perfectly honest with you. I'm very sceptical about this whole thing."

"That's perfectly understandable. Hopefully, I'll be able to put your mind at ease on any reservations you might have. Why don't you take a seat, and I'll do my best to answer all of your questions?"

"Okay."

"Would you like a drink? I only have tea, I'm afraid."

"Tea will be fine. Milk and one and two-thirds spoonfuls of sugar, please."

"One and — err — two — err? Right. I won't be a minute."

He disappeared into the back again, and returned with what proved to be a delicious cup of tea. He'd managed to get the sugar quota just right.

"I have to say, Scott, I find it hard to believe that there's such a thing as a model agency just for dogs."

"As far as I'm aware, this is the only one in Candlefield, but I'm sure there must be some in the human world."

"I didn't think there would be that much call for dog models."

"How many adverts featuring dogs have you seen in magazines or on TV?"

"I don't know. A lot, I suppose."

"Do you think that the businesses, who spend huge sums of money to advertise their products, want any old mutt to be the face of their company?"

"I'd never really thought about it."

"They most definitely do not. They want handsome dogs such as Barry to represent them."

"And these advertisers? They come to you?"

"Most of them, yes. Without wishing to blow my own trumpet, I've built something of a reputation in the business. They know if they contact me that they'll get only the very best. That's why I'm very selective about which dogs I approach."

"How long have you been doing this?"

"I started Pooch First eight years ago, but I've worked in the modelling business for almost twenty years. Between you and me, I much prefer working with dogs. They're far less temperamental than sups."

"What does it cost?"

"The advertiser? That depends entirely on the campaign they have in mind."

"I meant the dog owner. What would it cost me?"

"Nothing, of course."

"I thought there might be some charge for taking photos or something like that?"

"Certainly not. You should run away from any agency which wants you to give them money. I only make money if you do."

"I don't imagine that there's much money to be made. Do most people sign up just for the thrill of seeing their dog in a magazine or on screen?"

"I think you might be pleasantly surprised. I only deal with major advertisers; it isn't worth my time to get involved with the smaller accounts."

"What sort of money are we talking?"

"The very least you should expect to make from a campaign is five-hundred pounds."

"Five hundred?" I tried not to look as excited as I was. "From a single campaign?"

"Yes, and often it's more than that."

"Right. I had no idea."

"So? Is it something you'd be interested in?"

"I think so." Just try stopping me. "Not for the money of course, but because Barry seems so keen."

"Great. I'll need you to sign a contract, and then we have to get Barry over to my photographer."

"Sounds good."

"Where shall I send the contract?"

"Can you post it to an address in the human world?"

"Sure. That's no problem."

I gave him my office address, and he said he'd be in touch with details of the photoshoot.

Back on the street, I was feeling pretty pleased with life. At five-hundred pounds per gig, I stood to make a small fortune. Good old Barry.

I made a quick call to Aunt Lucy.

"It's me. I've just been to the dog model agency. It looks like they're legit. Will you tell Barry that I've agreed for him to sign with them, and that he'll need to get his photographs taken for his portfolio. I'll let you have the details when I know more."

"That's great, Jill. Barry will be thrilled. I don't imagine they pay very much, though?"

"No, but it isn't about the money. I'm just glad to do it for Barry."

What? Of course that was my only motivation. Just how mercenary do you think I am? Sheesh!

***

My income was about to increase dramatically, courtesy of Barry, so I figured I could give myself the rest of the afternoon off. And besides, I still had to work out how I was going to resolve the Dexter situation.

On my way home, I called in at the corner shop where Little Jack Corner was stocking the shelves behind the counter.

"I see you're buying custard creams again, Jill."

"I wouldn't want to run out."

"Very wise. I heard on the grapevine that there's a countrywide shortage of them."

"What? That's terrible."

"It's okay. I'm only pulling your leg."

"Don't do that. You had me going there for a minute. I see you've taken down all the mirrors. How come?"

"A couple of customers were dazzled by the beams of light; one lady walked straight into the display of pickled onions."

"Was she okay?"

"Yeah. A bit smelly, but otherwise unscathed."

"I suppose that means you and Missy are back to shouting to one another?"

"Not at all." He reached under the counter and brought out a walkie-talkie. "Corner One to Corner Two, come in."

Missy's voice came crackling through. "Corner Two receiving loud and clear."

"Just testing. Corner One over and out."

"Is she over by the buckets?" I said.

"The buckets have gone."

"All of them?"

"Yes." He looked very pleased with himself. "Every last one."

"How come? Did you have a run on them?"

"Not exactly. I sold them all to the same two people. I shouldn't talk about my customers behind their backs, but these two were a little strange. They were both wearing balaclavas."

***

Jack and I were seated at the kitchen table, eating pizza.

"Are you sure you heard correctly?" he said.

"Yes, Little Jack said they'd bought all sixty-seven buckets."

"Why would anyone need sixty-seven buckets?"

"Beats me. I thought the balaclava twins were weird before, but this confirms it."

Jack pinched the last slice of pizza just before I could grab it.

"That was mine."

"No, it wasn't. You've already had one more slice than me."

"Are you sure?"

"Positive.

"I wouldn't want you to feel guilty that I'm still hungry."

"That's okay. I don't." He grinned. "It's a pity you have to go out tonight."

"I have no choice. There's someone I need to interview who can only see me tonight."

"Shame. The semi-finals of the National Ten-Pin bowling are on TV."

"And there was I thinking you wanted to make mad, passionate love to me."

"We could have done that after the programme had finished."

"It's nice to know you have your priorities right."

"What is it you're working on tonight?"

"A cold case. A murder."

"Have you made much progress?"

"Not a lot." I checked my watch. "I'd better get going. Enjoy your bowling."

When I got into the car, my phone beeped with a text message from Dexter:

Jill. I'm worried sick. Don't know what to do.

I replied:

Take Jules to hospital at seven. I'll send you further instructions soon.

When I arrived at the hospital, the first thing I had to do was to find a doctor's coat, so I'd be able to wander around without being challenged.

Once I'd located the staff room, I made myself invisible and slipped inside. In there, I found a pile of white coats, presumably waiting to go to the laundry. It took me a couple of minutes to find one that was my size that wasn't covered in yucky stains.

After reversing the 'invisible' spell, I emerged from the staff room, looking every bit the doctor. No one gave me a second glance as I wandered from floor to floor, until I eventually found what I was looking for.

The bed was made, but the room was deserted. So too were the rooms on either side. The nearest nurses' station was at the far end of the corridor. This would be ideal.

I shot off a text to Dexter:

Bring Jules to room 3112 on the third floor.

He didn't reply, so I just had to hope that he'd seen it. There wasn't much time to spare because, by my calculations, he and Jules would be arriving within the next fifteen minutes.

The next step in my ingenious plan was to cast one of my least favourite spells: the 'ageing' spell. A quick check in the mirror confirmed that it had worked. Staring back at me was the same old woman who had helped to recover my mother's ring when it had been stolen in the care home.

Only then did it occur to me that I didn't have a nightdress. It was too late to go in search of one, so I slipped off the doctor's coat, threw it into a drawer, and then climbed into bed, fully dressed. If I made sure to keep the bed sheets up under my chin, no one should notice.

A few minutes later, the door opened, and in walked Dexter, followed by Jules. His face was a picture.

"Dexter," I said in a weak voice. "Come in. Who's that with you?"

"Hello—err—Gran. This is Jules."

"Hello, young lady. Come a little closer so that I can see you properly."

Jules followed Dexter over to the bed.

"Hello, Mrs Ribery. I brought these for you." Jules held up a small bouquet of flowers.

"How very kind. Put them on there, would you? I'll ask the nurse to get a vase."

"How are you feeling, Mrs Ribery?"

"Much better now, but still very weak."

"I hope you don't mind me coming here with Dexter?"

"Not at all. He told me that he'd left you stranded yesterday. That was very inconsiderate of him."

"It's okay. Once I knew why he'd had to shoot off, I completely understood."

"He's a little darling really, aren't you Dexter?"

"Thanks, Gran." He blushed.

Mission accomplished. I'd give it another couple of minutes, and then I'd tell my visitors that I was getting tired, and that I needed them to leave. Then it would be back home to Jack and a night of passion (always assuming the ten-pin bowling had finished).

"Mrs Wiseman?" A nurse appeared in the doorway. "We weren't expecting you for another hour. When did they bring you up?"

Jules turned to Dexter, and I saw her mouth the word,

Wiseman?

Before I could say anything, the nurse continued, "I'm afraid you two will have to leave now. Is this your gran?"

Dexter nodded.

"Say your goodbyes, please. It's time for your gran's bed bath."

Oh bum!

"Bye, Gran." Dexter started for the door.

"Aren't you going to give your gran a kiss?" The nurse called him back.

"Err — yeah — of course." He came over and gave me a peck on the cheek. I'm not sure which one of us felt more uncomfortable.

"Bye," Jules said, and then they both disappeared out of the door.

"They seem like nice kids." The nurse came to my bedside.

"No bed bath."

"Sorry?"

"I don't want a bed bath, thank you."

"Don't be silly. You know the routine. It will only take a few minutes."

I tried to stop her pulling back the sheets, but my frail old arms were no match for hers.

"What the — ?" She gasped when she saw that I was fully dressed.

I had to act quickly, so I cast the 'forget' spell, reversed the 'ageing' spell, and then hightailed it out of the room. The lift doors had just opened, so I caught a ride down to the ground floor.

That had been a close call, but I'd got away with it.

"Jill?"

I spun around to see Jules and Dexter. They must have taken the stairs.

"Jules? Hi. What are you doing here?"

"We've just been to see Dexter's gran, haven't we?"

Dexter nodded. He looked more than a little confused, and was probably still trying to work out who the old lady playing his grandmother was.

"How is she?" I asked.

"Tell her, Dexter," Jules prompted him.

"She — err — she's much better, thank you."

"That's great."

"What are you doing here, Jill?" Jules said.

"Me? I — err — I work here as a volunteer a few times each week."

"You've never mentioned it."

"I don't like to make a big thing of it, but I do like to do my bit for the community. Anyway, I'd better press on. They'll be expecting me up on the wards."

"Bye, Jill," Jules said, and then walked out, arm in arm with Dexter.

The sacrifices I made for my staff.

Chapter 9

The next morning, Jack and I were both in the kitchen. He'd made bacon cobs for the two of us, and I have to say that mine was going down a treat.

"Last night was fantastic," he said, and then wiped a splodge of ketchup from the side of his mouth.

"It sure was, Stud."

"I meant the bowling. Who would have thought the Titans would get through to the final?"

I glared at him.

"What? I'm only joking." He came over, grabbed me around the waist and lifted me off my feet. "Give me a kiss, sexy."

"You've still got some ketchup on your—"

Too late. He'd already planted his ketchupy lips on mine.

After that brief moment of passion, Jack went back to his bacon cob.

"I still can't get my head around those weirdos across the road, buying sixty-seven buckets," he said.

Neither could I. It was high time I checked out the balaclava twins. "I sometimes think you and I are the only normal people on this street."

He gave me a look. "There's nothing *normal* about you."

"What do you mean?"

"I don't mean that in a bad way. I like that you're totally kooky. That's one of the things that attracted me to you."

"And there was I thinking it was my looks, great body and personality."

"Those too, but the truth is, I've never met anyone else

quite like you. It's like you don't live in the same world as the rest of us. I don't really know how to explain it."

"In that case, don't try. Just give me another kiss instead."

"I love you, Jill Gooder."

"What brought that on?"

"What do you mean? Aren't I allowed to tell you that I love you?"

"Of course you are."

"This is the point where you're supposed to say it too."

"Say what?"

He rolled his eyes.

"Oh, right. Yes, of course, I love you."

"Wow, I'm overwhelmed."

"I *do* love you. You know I do."

"Enough to spend the rest of your life with me?"

"Where did that come from?"

"We never talk about the future."

"And you think that while we're eating bacon cobs would be the time to start?"

"This is what you always do."

"What do you mean?"

"Change the subject, or turn everything into a joke."

"No, I don't. Is that the time? I have to get going. I promised that I'd—err—drop in on Kathy. I'll see you tonight."

I grabbed my coat and bag, and hightailed it out of the house before he could ask any more awkward questions. I loved Jack more than life itself, but I didn't know how to hold the kind of conversation he clearly wanted to have. I really wanted to tell him that we'd be together forever—I truly hoped we would. But it wasn't as simple as that—not even close. He had no idea who I was—not really. There was a major part of my life that he knew nothing about.

Megan was standing behind her van. The back doors were open, and she was spraying the interior with what appeared to be air freshener.

"Hi, Jill."

"Morning. Thanks again for the lift yesterday."

"No problem. I'm just trying to get rid of the smell in here. It's as though something crept inside and died."

"How did the job go yesterday?"

"Okay, thanks, but it took a little longer than I expected. Is your car alright now?"

"Yeah. All sorted."

"Do you read The Bugle, Jill?"

"Not if I can help it, but Jack does buy it for the bowling scores, occasionally."

"Did you see the headline yesterday? About the zombies?"

"Yeah. They'll print any old rubbish."

"That's what I thought, but at the house where I was working yesterday, the woman reckoned her brother-in-law had seen one. He lives not far from here."

"That explains it."

"Explains what?"

"The smell in your van. Maybe a zombie climbed inside."

She smiled. "Makes you think, though, doesn't it? Who knows what might be living alongside us."

"True. For all you know, I might really be a witch."

She laughed. "That can't be true, or you would have used magic to mend your car yesterday."

***

Today was the day that Kathy was supposed to hand in her notice at Ever. Maria had already left to go and work with Luther, so Grandma wouldn't be very thrilled when she found out that Kathy was jumping ship too.

Kathy was behind the tea room counter, daydreaming.

"Have you done the deed yet?" I asked.

"Do you have to sneak up on people like that?"

"Sorry. I didn't realise you were sleeping. So? Have you?"

"Not yet. I'm working myself up to it."

"Just do it."

"That's easy for you to say. I barely slept last night, wondering how she'll react."

"She'll probably be glad to see the back of a slacker like you."

"Thanks a lot. Did you actually want something, or did you just come in to insult me and gloat at my discomfort?"

"Mainly that, but also to ask if Jack has said anything to you about him and me recently."

"Like what in particular?"

"Anything."

"What's this all about, Jill?"

"Just now, he asked how I saw our future. What kind of question is that?"

"OMG, he wants to get married."

"Whoa there! Where did you get that from? That's not

what he meant at all. And who over the age of seventeen says: OMG?"

"Of course that's what he was talking about. What did you say?"

"Nothing really. I couldn't figure out why he was asking such deep questions over breakfast. He even had the audacity to accuse me of avoiding any kind of serious conversation."

"What did you say to that?"

"That I had to leave because I'd promised to drop in on you."

Kathy rolled her eyes. "You kind of proved his point for him then, didn't you?"

"I still don't think he was talking about marriage."

"It's as plain as day."

"Not to me."

"Perhaps not, but it would be to any normal human being. That must be it. Maybe you're not human. Maybe Mum and Dad didn't adopt you at all. Maybe they had you manufactured at the robot works."

Just then, an almighty banging sound started up, under our feet.

"What's that?"

Kathy shrugged. "It's been going on for a few days. It starts about this time, and continues all day."

"Does Grandma know about it?"

"Of course she does. She'd have to be stone deaf not to."

"What does she have to say about it?"

"Nothing. It's almost as though she already knows what it is."

"Has she said as much?"

"No. When I asked her, she just gave me the brush off

as usual. She never tells me anything. That's another reason I won't be sorry to see the back of this place."

"I suppose I'd better get going. Good luck with the resignation."

"Thanks. I have a feeling I'm going to need it."

***

Mrs V had yet more brochures spread across her desk.

"Morning, Mrs V."

"Morning, dear. What do you think of Seychelles?"

"I'm not really into all that crustacean stuff. You'd be better speaking to Betty Longbottom; she's the expert."

"Not sea shells. *Seychelles*. Armi and I have been thinking about our honeymoon."

"Oh, right. I've never been there. To be honest, I'm not that keen on travelling abroad. It's too much like hard work, and then there's all that heat. Oh, by the way, I have some news that might interest you."

"What's that?"

"Kathy is handing in her notice at Ever today. Unless she loses her nerve, that is."

"Has she found herself another job?"

"No. She's opening her own shop, and you'll never guess what it's going to be?"

"Is it a millinery shop? I've often said that Washbridge is poorly served for hats."

"No. It's a bridal shop."

That got Mrs V's attention.

"Really? How very exciting. When will it open?"

"I don't know. They haven't even found premises yet, but it should be open in plenty of time for you and Armi."

"What's she going to call it?"

"Kathy's Bridal Shop."

"That's a great name, but then she always did have a wonderful imagination."

Huh?

"Mrs V, can I ask you a question?"

"As long as it doesn't involve geometry. I was never very good with shapes."

"Err—no, it's not geometry. Hypothetically speaking, if Armi was to say that he wanted to talk about the future, what would you think he meant?"

"That's exactly what he did say. Just before he proposed."

Oh bum!

"What's up with you?" Winky said, as soon as I walked into my office. "You look like you've just—err—I was going to say: seen a ghost, but you do that all the time. What's wrong?"

"Nothing. I've just had a bit of a shock."

"Did they put up the price of custard creams again? I can remember how traumatised you were the last time."

"No, nothing like that. Jack might be about to ask me to marry him."

"That can't be right. Not even he's that crazy."

"What do you mean? Why wouldn't he want to marry me?"

"You're pretty weird."

"I'm not."

"You talk to cats."

"That doesn't make me weird."

"You're a witch."

"There is that."

"You should come clean and tell him."

"That I'm a witch? I can't. The rogue retrievers would take me back to Candlefield."

"Only if they found out."

"I can't take that risk."

"Coward."

"Shut up. I didn't ask for your opinion anyway."

"Fair enough. Just don't forget you're taking me to the Will reading later."

***

Just after eleven, Mrs V popped her head in the door.

"There's a Mr Dewey here, Jill. He wonders if you might spare him a minute."

"Certainly. Send him in, would you?"

I'd first heard of Stewey Dewey from Harry and Larry who ran Spooky Wooky, a tea room in Ghost Town. For a long time, they'd believed that Stewey had been responsible for their deaths, but I'd discovered that he had in fact injured himself trying to rescue them. Now the three of them were good friends, and the last I'd heard, they were going to open a new bakery here in Washbridge.

"Stewey, good to see you again."

"You too, Jill. Thanks for sparing me a few minutes."

"Have you come to tell me that the bakery is open, and I can claim my free muffins for life?"

"If all goes to plan, we should open within a month." He laughed. "Of course, you realise I was joking about the muffins for life?"

Joking? Nooo!

"Yes, of course." I forced a smile. This day was going from bad to worse. "What brings you here today?"

"We're planning the grand opening, but we've got a bit of a problem, which we're hoping you might be able to help us with."

Sheesh! He tramples all over my muffin dreams and now he wants my help?

"If I can, I will."

"The thing is, Harry and Larry really want to be present at the grand opening."

"I should think so too. What's stopping them? Surely they can get someone to look after Spooky Wooky for a few hours, can't they?"

"That's not the problem. They want to *really* be there, if you know what I mean?"

"Sorry. You've lost me."

"They want other people to be able to see them, so they can join in with the celebrations. As I understand it, they can attach themselves to me, but then I'd be the only one who could see them. They thought that you might know of some way to help them."

"The Spookberry potion would do what they want, but it's only available under licence. Even if they could get hold of some, I don't see how it would help."

"How do you mean?"

"Don't you think it might alarm people if they just turn up out of the blue? They're supposed to be dead."

"They were planning to wear disguises, and to use make-up so they looked less—err—ghostlike, but if we can't find a way for everyone to see them, there's no point."

"I have a few contacts over in GT. I'll ask around to see if there's any way they would be able to get a licence for Spookberry, just for the grand opening."

"Would you, Jill? That would be fantastic."

"Don't make any promises to Harry and Larry. I'd hate to build up their hopes in case I'm unable to deliver."

***

"Come on! Hurry up! We'll be late." Winky was pacing back and forth.

"There's plenty of time. The solicitor's office is only a couple of minutes from here. I still don't think it's a good idea for you to come with me."

"I'm going with you, and that's all there is to it."

"Okay, on your head be it." I went over to the cupboard, and took out the cat basket.

"I'm not getting in that thing."

"You have to. I can hardly walk in there with you in my arms, can I?"

"I suppose not." He climbed into the basket. "The indignity of it all."

"Where are you taking the cat, Jill?" Mrs V looked up from her holiday brochures.

"I—err—I'm just taking him to the vets for flea treatment."

"Manky old thing. I don't know why you put up with him."

"I don't have fleas," Winky said, as we made our way downstairs. "Why didn't you tell her where we're really going?"

"I'm not sure she would have understood. I'm not even sure that I do."

The offices of Blake, Lake and Makepiece were close to those of my old friends: Armitage, Armitage, Armitage and Poole.

"Hi. I'm here for the reading of the Shoesmith Will."

"What's that?" The receptionist pointed at the basket.

"It's a cat."

"It's only got one eye."

"Really?" I glanced around the floor. "It must have fallen out."

"Very amusing. Why have you brought it with you?"

"He's one of the beneficiaries of the Will."

"He can't come in here."

"But he's one of the benef—"

"It doesn't matter. No animals are allowed. Are you his owner?"

"In a manner of speaking."

"Then you can go through, but you'll have to leave the cat outside."

"What if he gets eaten by a dog?"

She shrugged; she was obviously a cat lover.

"Sorry, Winky," I said, once we were back outside. "I'll leave you in this alleyway. You should be safe here."

"No chance. I'm coming in with you."

"You heard what the woman said."

"Make me invisible."

"What?"

"You're a witch, aren't you? Make me invisible, and carry me inside."

"Don't you think that might look a little odd?"

"Not if you put me in your bag."

"It's not big enough."

"Of course it is. That handbag of yours is enormous. Just don't close it."

"I'm not sure about this."

"Come on. We'll miss the reading."

Something told me I was going to regret this, but I took him out of the basket, cast the 'hide' spell, and put him in my handbag.

"See, no cat," I said to the receptionist, who was probably trying to work out why my handbag was gaping open.

Inside the solicitor's office, several people were seated on the two rows of chairs that had been laid out in front of the desk.

"When's it going to start?" Winky whispered.

"Be quiet. You mustn't speak."

"Pardon?" The woman two seats away looked puzzled.

"Nothing. Sorry."

Five minutes later, the solicitor took his seat. "Ladies and gentlemen—"

"And cat," Winky chipped in.

"Be quiet!" I shushed him.

"Thank you for coming in today. I will now read the last Will and Testament of Roland Shoesmith: To my two darling daughters, Coral and Laurel, I leave two million pounds each."

"Two million?" Winky gasped. "I told you he was rich."

"Shut up!"

"Pardon?" The solicitor looked at me.

"Sorry, I just sneezed."

The reading of the Will took almost thirty minutes. Winky was right about one thing: Shoesmith had been loaded. In total, I calculated he had left at least nine million pounds to various relatives, friends and charities.

"And finally, to my long-lost cat, Marmaduke, who I was forced to give up for adoption, I bequeath the collar he wore when he belonged to me." The solicitor looked up. "That concludes the reading of the Will."

"A grotty old collar?" Winky said. "Is that all I get for all my pain and distress?"

"Marmaduke?" I laughed.

"What?"

"You were called Marmaduke."

"Who cares?"

"I think you should revert to your original name. Marmaduke suits you."

"Shut up. I want to go home."

I was just on my way out of the door when someone called me back. It was the snotty receptionist.

"You forgot this." She was holding a large brown envelope at arm's length, as though it was full of something unspeakable. "It's the collar."

"Right. Thanks."

After reversing the 'hide' spell, we made our way back to the office.

Once there, Winky jumped out of the basket, and disappeared under the sofa to sulk.

"You forgot your collar, Marmaduke."

"You can keep it."

"No, it's yours." I pushed the envelope under the sofa. "And don't worry. You can keep my twenty percent cut."

Snigger.

Chapter 10

Poor old Winky, or should I say Marmaduke? He'd been so sure that he was going to inherit a small fortune, but all he'd ended up with was a tatty old collar. I shouldn't laugh because I'd stood to collect twenty percent of his inheritance, but then I'd never really expected it to amount to anything.

Marmaduke? LOL.

What? If Kathy can say OMG, then I can say LOL.

It turned out that the current concierge at the Nexler Building was the same one who'd worked there at the time of Stephen Bradley's murder. His name was Lucas Broad, and he'd agreed to speak to me.

There was only one man seated behind the huge reception desk on the ground floor. Dressed in an immaculate navy-blue suit, he greeted me with a smile.

"Good afternoon, madam."

"Lucas?"

"No, I'm Joe. Can I help?"

"Actually, Lucas is expecting me. Is he around?"

"I can get him for you. What's your name, please?"

"Jill Gooder."

Joe disappeared through a door marked 'Private', and returned moments later, trailed by a taller man who was wearing an identical suit.

"Hi, I'm Lucas."

"Thanks for seeing me at such short notice."

"No problem. There's a meeting room over there where we can talk."

He led the way across the large reception hall, and then

held open the meeting room door for me. "Please take a seat. There's water if you'd like some."

"I'm okay, thanks. As I mentioned on the phone, I'd like to talk to you about Stephen Bradley's death."

He nodded. "I'm happy to answer any questions you may have."

"Had you been working here long when it happened?"

"A little over six months. I'd just completed my probation period."

"I realise that it's a long time ago, but I'm hoping you might still remember the events of that day."

"I'm never likely to forget them. It's without doubt the worst day of my career to-date. I still feel responsible."

"Why do you say that?"

"I was the only one on the desk that night, so it was up to me to monitor who came into the building. The murderer must have got past me somehow, but I still have no idea how."

"Did your employer blame you?"

"No, but that doesn't stop me feeling like it was my fault."

"You're assuming that the murderer came from outside the building. Isn't it possible that it was actually someone who worked here?"

"There were very few people in the building around the time that the murder took place. The police interviewed everyone who was here, and cleared them all."

"Did the building have CCTV installed back then?"

"Yes. There were cameras on every door on the ground floor: front, back and side. No one could get in or out of the building without being caught on it."

"I assume the police studied it?"

"Yes. Everyone who was seen entering the building could be accounted for."

"What about Thomas Bradley? Stephen's partner?"

"He was caught on CCTV leaving the building before the murder took place."

"I didn't think they had an exact time of death. How could the police be sure that Stephen Bradley wasn't already dead before Thomas left?"

"Because Stephen was caught on one of the internal CCTV cameras, sometime after Thomas had left the building."

"Where was he seen?"

"There were internal cameras on some of the fire doors. Stephen Bradley walked past one, on his way to the toilet."

"Did you know Stephen Bradley?"

"Only to say good morning or good night to. Like I said, I hadn't been in the job very long at the time."

"Do you have any theories as to what might have happened?"

"No, but it isn't through lack of trying. I've been over the events of that night a million times, and I must have watched the CCTV almost as many times. I'm still no wiser."

"I appreciate you taking time out of your day to talk to me." I handed him my card. "Would you call me if you think of anything else? Anything at all."

"Sure."

I stood up and started for the door.

"I still have the DVD, you know," he said.

"Sorry?"

"When the murder was reported, I copied the day's

CCTV footage, so I'd be able to study it at home. I've watched it so many times that I've almost worn out the disc."

"Where is it?"

"At my place. I haven't looked at it for years, but I couldn't bring myself to throw it away, just in case. Would you like to see it?"

"Yes, please. If you bring it in, I'll pick it up from you the next time I'm passing."

***

I'd no sooner left the Nexler Building than my phone rang.

"Jill, it's Alicia."

"Hi."

"I've discovered where all those witches are working. The ones that Ma Chivers recruited."

"I'm listening."

"They're in a small industrial unit on the Flawton Industrial Estate. Do you know it?"

"No."

"It's a couple of miles outside Washbridge. Just off the main road to West Chipping."

"What has she got them doing?"

"I don't know. I daren't go near the place because if she sees me, I'll be done for. I'm going to try to speak to some of the witches who are working there. If I have any luck, I'll let you know."

"Okay, thanks."

What was I supposed to make of the 'new' Alicia? Had

she really turned over a new leaf? I still had my doubts. I would have to be on my guard because this could all be an elaborate charade designed to gain my trust.

***

I figured that the best person to ask about Spookberry licences would be Constance Bowler. She'd agreed to spare me a few minutes, so I magicked myself over to her office in Ghost Town.

"Thanks for seeing me, Constance."

"No problem. It's been a quiet week so far. Not that I'm complaining."

"I wanted to ask you about Spookberry licences."

"What about them?"

"Larry and Harry who run the Spooky Wooky tea room have entered into a joint venture with someone in the human world."

"How did that come about?"

"It's a long story, but basically Harry and Larry used to be rivals with a guy named Stewey Dewey. Before they died, that is."

"Right."

"I'm not sure if you know, but Harry and Larry died in a fire, which for many years they believed Stewey had set. It turned out that he hadn't, and in fact, he'd been injured trying to save them. The three of them are now the best of friends."

"Hence the new venture?"

"Exactly. Harry and Larry want to attend the grand opening in the human world."

"Can't they just attach themselves to this Dewey

character?"

"They can, but they'd like the other people present to be able to see them."

"I think I see where this is going. Spookberry?"

"That's right. Stewey asked if I could help. I told them that they'd need a licence and said I'd ask you how they could go about getting one."

"They're out of luck, I'm afraid. It's my understanding that licences aren't granted to individuals or for 'one-off' events such as this. They're only granted to businesses who have legitimate reasons to need them for their interactions with the human world."

"That's a little disappointing."

"To be honest, I think it's a poorly thought out policy. In fact, it's that very policy that is the reason for the black market trade in Spookberry. If the authorities would lighten up on the restrictions, the crooks selling it would be put out of business. And of course, there's no quality control for the product sold on the black market. There have been quite a few horror stories, I can tell you. Harry and Larry will need to find a licensed business that would be willing to help out."

"My friend, the colonel, recently took over Hauntings Unlimited. Maybe he can help."

"It's certainly worth a try."

"Thanks, Constance."

***

I'd tried to phone the colonel, but he wasn't picking up; he was probably busy with his new business venture. I'd just have to go back to my office, which had been one of the first places he'd visited after he 'came back' as a ghost, and try calling his name from there.

***

Mrs V was still poring over the holiday brochures.

"Any messages, Mrs V?"

"No, but I did get a call from Jules."

"Is she okay?"

"Yes, she sounded very pleased with life. Apparently, she and her new young man had a bit of a falling out, but everything's okay now. I feel sorry for the young people of today. All this total media can't be good for them."

"*Total media*?" I had no idea what she was talking about, but then it clicked. "Hang on. You mean *social*. It's *social* media."

"It's not something we had to worry about in our day, is it?"

In *our* day? Just how old did she think I was?

"Have you decided where to go on honeymoon yet?"

"Not yet. Armi suggested a cruise."

"That might be nice."

"I'm not too keen. There's a bit too much water for my liking."

I was expecting Winky still to be sulking, but I couldn't have been any more wrong. He was sitting on my desk, and next to him was a half-empty bottle of champagne.

"Jill!" He hiccupped. "Would you care to join me in a toast?"

"Are you drunk?"

"A little merry, perhaps." He poured out another glass,

and offered it to me.

"No, thanks. I know you're disappointed about the inheritance, but drinking to drown your sorrows is not the solution."

"I'm not drowning my sorrows; I'm celebrating."

"What's that?" I pointed to the watch he was wearing.

"Do you like it?"

"It's very—never mind that. Where did you get it? You didn't steal it, did you?"

"Of course not. What do you think I am?"

"You'd better not have maxed out my credit card."

"Your credit limit isn't high enough to pay for this little beauty."

"So how did you get it?"

"I bought it of course. With part of my inheritance."

"Now I know you're drunk. The only thing you inherited was a collar."

"Would that be the *diamond-encrusted* collar that I sold a couple of hours ago? You wouldn't believe how much I got for it."

"*Diamonds*?" It had never even occurred to me to look at the collar. That didn't matter though because I stood to gain anyway. "Where's my twenty percent cut?"

"What twenty percent?"

"That's what we agreed before I took you to the solicitors."

"That's true, but when we got back, and I was under the sofa, do you remember what you said?"

I cast my mind back, and then it hit me like a ton of bricks. In a moment of madness, I'd said: *And don't worry. You can keep my twenty percent cut.*

"You're not really going to hold me to that, are you?"

"What do you think?" He grinned.

"I hate you. Marmaduke."

"Sticks and stones may break my bones, but diamonds are a cat's best friend."

"That's not even a saying. And you can get off my desk."

Twenty minutes later, Winky had fallen asleep on the sofa, so I took the bottle of champagne away from him. He'd had more than enough to drink for one day.

That watch of his must have cost at least five grand. Just how much had he made from the sale of those diamonds? I don't imagine I'll ever find out.

How was it that he always came out smelling of roses while I always ended up smelling like I'd been rolling in cow dung?

"Colonel? Priscilla? Are you there?"

No reply.

I tried again, "Colonel? Priscilla?"

The temperature dropped, and the colonel appeared.

"You called, Jill? Are we celebrating something?"

"Sorry?"

"The champers?"

"This isn't mine. It's—err—never mind. I wanted to ask you a favour."

"Ask away, young lady."

"Does Hauntings Unlimited have a Spookberry licence?"

"We do, for all the good it does."

"How do you mean?"

"I take it you know that Spookberry should only be

distributed through licensed businesses?"

"Yes, that's actually why I wanted to talk to you."

"The licensing system is not being policed effectively, and it's having a detrimental effect on our business."

"How come?"

"Ghosts who want to find work in the human world normally use companies such as ours because that should be the only way they can gain access to Spookberry. But now, there's some charlatan going around, selling unlicensed Spookberry. That means that ghosts no longer need us. We're struggling to keep workers on our books."

"I'm sorry to hear that, Colonel. Can't the police help?"

"It's actually overseen by the licensing authorities who are next to useless. The police refuse to get involved."

"The guy who is selling the unlicensed Spookberry, is his name Homer Range, by any chance?"

"That's right. How did you know?"

"I heard about him from a couple of ghosts who were haunting the maze at Washbridge Country Hall. Do you know Harry and Larry from Spooky Wooky?"

"Of course. It's the best tea room in GT."

"They need to get hold of some licensed Spookberry so they can attend the grand opening of a bakery here in Washbridge. If you could see your way clear to helping them out, then I'll do my best to put Mr Homer Range out of business. How does that sound?"

"Like a top-notch plan."

"Great. I'll tell Harry and Larry you'll be in touch, shall I?"

"Please do. Priscilla and I are regular visitors to Spooky Wooky, so I'll sort them out the next time I'm in there."

***

I didn't want to be around when Winky woke up because there was only so much gloating I could take in one day.

"I'm calling it a day, Mrs V. I've got a bit of a headache."

"It'll be all that champagne. I saw the bottle when I brought your tea in."

"That isn't—err—I didn't—never mind. I'll see you next week."

"Are you sure you should be driving?"

I couldn't be bothered to stick around to explain. Even if I had, what would I have said? That the champagne belonged to Winky AKA Marmaduke, who had just done me out of my share of a small fortune in diamonds?

Mrs V didn't need to hear that. No one did.

Great! I was halfway to the car park when the heavens decided to open, and of course, I'd left my umbrella in the house. The sooner I got home to my custard creams, the better.

By the time I reached the car, I looked like a drowned rat. Surely, nothing else could go wrong.

Spoke too soon.

The queue at the toll bridge was as long as I'd ever seen it. Ten minutes later, and I hadn't moved even an inch. This was crazy. I needed to find out what was going on, and as I was already soaked to the skin, walking down to the pay booth wasn't going to make much difference.

As I got closer, I could see that the man in the car at the front of the queue was remonstrating with Mr Ivers.

"What's going on?" I demanded.

"It's this idiot!" the man in the car shouted.

"What's wrong, Mr Ivers?" I said.

"Andy's stuck."

"Sorry?"

He gestured to the mechanical arm. "It seems to be stuck. I think it must be the rain."

"Why don't you just take the cash by hand?"

"I thought I could get Andy working again."

I leaned into the booth, so that my face was inches from his. "Do I look as though I've had a good day, Mr Ivers?"

"You do seem a little upset. And you're rather wet."

"You're right on both counts. And do you know what this is?" I tapped the mechanical arm. "This is the straw. The last one that broke the camel's back. Now, let me tell you what's going to happen. You're going to start taking the cash by hand."

"But my elbows are—"

"I don't want to hear another word about your elbows or about Andy. The only sound I want to hear is the clinking of coins as you collect them. Got it?"

"Okay, but if my elbows—"

"What did I just say?"

As I turned away from the booth, the man in the car winked at me. "Has anyone ever told you you're incredibly hot when you get angry?"

Chapter 11

Sunday was probably my favourite day of the week. Normally, if neither of us was working, we'd have a bit of a lie-in, and perhaps go out for lunch. But today Jack had been called into work, so I would have to find a way to amuse myself. I might take this opportunity to check out the balaclava twins and their stash of buckets.

The previous day had somehow turned into an all-day shopping expedition. Whoever it was that said women are the ones who love to shop, had obviously never met Jack. He'd wanted a new jumper and a pair of shoes, which by my reckoning should have taken an hour max.

Some chance!

It had taken him over two hours just to choose some shoes; he must have tried on thirty pairs. It wouldn't have been so bad if I could have left him to it, but he said he wanted me to stay so I could give my opinion. Towards the end, long after I'd lost the will to live, if he'd tried on a pair of fisherman's wading boots, I would have told him they looked good. When he eventually did choose a pair (the first pair he'd tried on two hours earlier, incidentally), I thought we were on the home straight, but I hadn't accounted for the jumper challenge ahead. Polo, round neck or v-neck? Black, blue or green? Wool, acrylic or a mix?

The next time he wanted to go clothes shopping, I was definitely going to remember an urgent case I had to work on.

One good thing did come out of the day, though. He didn't resurrect the subject of 'our future'. And thankfully, the 'M' word wasn't mentioned.

It was ten minutes after midday, and I'd just finished breakfast.

What? I totally deserved a lie-in after the week I'd just had.

As I was saying, I'd just finished my fry-up when there was a knock at the door.

"Blossom?"

"Good afternoon, Jill. I hope you don't mind my popping over, but I saw Jack go out earlier, and I thought you might like a bit of company. I know what it's like being a woman on her own."

Huh?

"Would you like to come in? I've just made a cup of tea."

"That would be lovely, dear. I'll only stay a few minutes because it's almost time for my lunch." She followed me into the kitchen. "Oh, I see you've already had yours?"

"This is actually my — err — yeah, I was a bit peckish so had an early lunch. Would you like a biscuit, Blossom?"

"I probably shouldn't. I don't want to spoil my appetite. Will Jack be gone long?"

"He's had to go into work. He'll probably be gone all day."

"What does he do?"

"He's a detective; he works out of West Chipping."

"Can I change my mind about that biscuit? Just one won't hurt, will it?"

"Sure."

I was halfway to the cupboard when there was a loud pounding at the door. When I spun around, Blossom was standing behind me.

"That sounds like it might be urgent, dear."

"Just a minute!" I hurried to the door, followed by Blossom.

"Clare? What's wrong?"

My next door neighbour looked as pale as a ghost.

"It's Tony." Was all she could manage before she dissolved into tears.

"Come in." I helped her inside.

"I think it would be best if I left you to it, dear," Blossom said. "I hope everything is alright."

"Okay, Blossom, thanks." I took Clare through to the lounge and settled her on the sofa. "What's wrong with Tony?"

"He's gone missing."

"Take a deep breath, and tell me exactly what's happened."

It took her a while to compose herself, but she eventually managed to tell the story.

"Do you remember that we told you he and I were going to different cons yesterday?"

"Yeah. AquaCon and — err — ?"

"VegCon. They were both one-day events. When I got back just before midnight, I expected Tony to be home because his con was much closer to Washbridge. When he wasn't, I waited up on the sofa, but I must have fallen asleep, and didn't wake until a couple of hours ago. He still isn't back, Jill."

"Have you tried to call him?"

"I've done nothing else since I woke up, but the message says the number I'm calling cannot be reached. I'm really worried, Jill."

"I'm sure he's okay."

"He would have called me if he'd been delayed."

"I don't want you to take this the wrong way, but the last time I saw the two of you, you were having words."

"That was nothing. We were just poking fun at each other's choice of con."

"Okay. What can I do to help?"

"I want to go to the Jamber Conference Centre where VegCon was held, but I don't have the car—Tony took it. I realise it's an imposition, but I was hoping that you might be able to drive me there. I know I could take a taxi, but I'm scared I might lose it and start blubbing."

"It's okay. Jack's at work and I don't have anything else planned. Give me a couple of minutes to get changed, and I'll meet you at the car."

"Thanks, Jill. I'll go and get my bag."

So much for my day of relaxation.

***

When we reached the toll bridge, I was relieved to see that Andy was working again. Mr Ivers saw me pop the cash onto the mechanical arm, but he didn't speak. He was no doubt still upset at my recent outburst—with a bit of luck, he'd never speak to me again.

Clare was very quiet on the drive to the Jamber Conference Centre, but at least she'd stopped crying.

"Have you been here before?" I asked.

"Just once. We came here for SausageCon last year."

"Right." Somehow, I managed not to laugh. "We're almost there."

The conference centre car park was locked, so we had to

park on a nearby side-street. I had no idea what Clare was hoping to find because the venue was obviously closed.

"Why don't you try his phone again?" I suggested, as we made our way to the building.

"I just did. It's still dead."

The main doors to the venue were locked, so we walked around the perimeter in the hope that we might find a security guard at one of the other exits, but there was no one to be seen. When we arrived back at the main doors, Clare sank down onto the steps, and began to sob.

"It's going to be alright." I put my hand on her shoulder. "Tony will be okay."

"How can you know that? Maybe he's been in a car crash." She wiped her eyes and nose. "That must be it. Nothing else makes any sense. I'm going to call the hospitals."

While Clare was on the phone, I decided to try something. I cast the 'listen' spell and focussed on the conference centre. I was hoping I might hear a security guard moving around inside, but instead I heard two voices: a man and a woman.

"Help! Please help us!"

"You're wasting your time. No one is out there."

"At least I'm trying to do something. You're just standing there like a useless carrot."

I recognised Tony's voice, but there was no way I could tell Clare what I'd just heard. How would I explain how I'd managed to hear him?

"How's it going, Clare?" I asked.

"They're checking, but there are other hospitals he could have been taken to."

"I'll take another look around the perimeter to see if I

can find a security guard."

She nodded, and then went back to the phone. "Yes, I'm still holding."

On our first lap of the building, I'd noticed that one of the exit doors opened onto a quiet side street, so I hurried back there. I would have liked to use the 'power' spell to force the doors, but I was worried that might set off an alarm. Instead, I used the spell that I would normally use to travel from one location to another. I only needed to transport myself a few yards — to the other side of the locked doors. I wasn't thrilled about gaining access this way because I had no clue what was on the other side of those doors, but it was Hobson's choice.

Gross!

Some idiot had left a giant bin just inside the doors, and I'd managed to magic myself inside of it. I was neck-deep in all manner of discarded food, packaging and empty plastic bottles.

It was a bit of a struggle, but I managed to lift the bin lid, and climb out. I looked and smelled disgusting, so I used the 'take-it-back' spell which worked on my clothes and shoes, but left my hair littered with all manner of rubbish. It took me several minutes to brush all the stuff from my hair.

I was conscious that Clare would soon come looking for me, so I had to get a sprint on. The man and woman I'd heard earlier were still squabbling, so I followed their voices to a service lift at the rear of the building. Once there, I no longer needed the 'listen' spell because I could hear the woman's calls without it.

"Please! Help us! Is anyone there?"

It didn't take a genius to work out that the lift was stuck, but I couldn't risk calling for help because then I'd have to explain how I'd gained access to the building. Before I went to their aid, I needed to disguise myself, so I used the 'doppelganger' spell to make myself look like Peter, complete with the overalls he normally wore. Then I cast the 'power' spell and forced open the lift doors.

"Thank goodness!" The woman screamed when she saw me. "Help us!"

The lift was stuck just below the floor I was on, so I could only see her from the shoulders upwards.

"Give me your hand."

I tried to pull her up, but she didn't seem to be helping much. Eventually, I managed it, and she popped out through the gap. It was only when she was out that I realised she was wearing a vegetable costume, which was peeled down to her waist. The bottom half of the costume still covered her legs, with just her feet poking out—no wonder it had been such a struggle for her to climb out of the lift.

"Broad bean?" I asked.

"Runner bean, actually."

"Never mind what kind of bean she is," Tony shouted. "Get me out of here."

It proved to be just as difficult to extract him because his legs were inside his carrot costume.

"I'd better call my wife," he said when he was out of the lift. "There was no signal in there."

"There's no need. She's the one who alerted us that you were missing. She's waiting outside for you."

On hearing that, and without saying a word, the woman pulled up her costume so that the top half of her body and head was covered, leaving just a small slot through which to see. It seemed a strange thing to do, but I didn't comment.

I still daren't open the exit doors in case the alarm went off, so I grabbed Tony and the woman by the hand, and before they could ask what I was doing, I magicked the three of us back outside. Fortunately, there was no one in the side street, so I quickly reversed the 'doppelganger' spell, and then cast the 'forget' spell on both of them.

"Jill?" Tony looked understandably confused. "What are you doing here?"

"Clare asked me to give her a lift."

"What happened to the man who rescued us?" the bean said. "I remember getting out of the lift, but everything after that is a blank."

"He brought you outside, and then he went back into the building."

Just then, Clare came running around the corner, but stopped dead in her tracks when she saw the three of us.

"Tony, where have you been? I was worried to death."

"We—err—I got stuck in the lift."

"How did you get out?"

Before Tony had the chance to reply, I jumped in, "I'll explain everything later. Let's get back to the car." I turned to the bean. "Can we give you a lift somewhere?"

"It's okay. I live just down the road."

"Wendy?" Clare glared at the bean.

The runner bean peeled back the top of her costume. "Hello, Clare."

"You two were stuck in the lift together?" Clare glanced between the carrot and the bean.

"I should go." The bean scurried away as fast as her

costume would allow.

"What's going on, Tony?" Clare demanded.

"I can explain."

Before he had the chance, I interrupted, "We really should get back to the car."

I climbed into the driver's seat; Clare and the carrot got into the back. As we drove home, my neighbours continued their 'discussion'.

"How could you?" Clare screamed at him.

"I didn't know Wendy would be at the con."

"You're lying. That's why you suggested I go to AquaCon, isn't it?"

"That's nonsense. Wendy and I split up years ago."

"You've never got over her, though, have you?"

"I had no idea she'd be here. I barely spoke two words to her all day."

"Why were you in a lift with her, then?"

"We were on our way out."

"In the *service* lift?"

"The others were busy."

"I'm not stupid, Tony. I know what you two were up to. And to think that I've made myself sick with worry."

"I tried to call you, but there was no signal in the lift, and the alarm button didn't work. It's a good thing that Jill managed to alert someone, or we might have been there until Monday morning."

"I bet you'd have liked that, wouldn't you? The chance to spend another night with that cow, Wendy Rathbone."

"Now you're just being silly. I was dressed as a carrot and she was dressed as a runner bean. What could we possibly get up to?"

The two of them were still at each other's throats when I dropped them home. I was exhausted, and no longer had the energy or inclination to investigate the balaclava twins. I'd had enough weirdness for one day.

**

When Jack got home, I was stretched out on the sofa in front of the TV, with a box of chocolates.

"I can see you've had a busy day." He grinned. "Any of those chocolates left?"

"Of course. Help yourself."

"Is that it? Turkish delight and hazelnut whirl?"

"I saved you some, didn't I?"

"Only because you don't like those two."

"Some people are never grateful."

"Have you been on that sofa all day?"

"I'll have you know I had to rescue a carrot and a runner bean who were stuck in a lift."

"It sounds like you've been at the wine too."

"I'm telling you the truth. Clare came around here in a panic because Tony hadn't come home from VegCon."

"*Vegcon*? What's that when it's at home?"

"It's exactly what it sounds like. Anyway, it turned out that Tony the carrot was trapped in a lift with a runner bean."

"Brilliant. You couldn't make this stuff up."

"You haven't heard the best of it yet. It seems that the runner bean was one of Tony's old flames."

"Oh dear."

"You should have heard the ear-bashing Clare gave him

on the drive back home. The next con they go to will probably be DivorceCon."

"Thank goodness we're not like those two." He bent down and gave me a peck on the cheek. "Have you changed your shampoo?"

"No. Why?"

"Your hair smells really — err — weird."

Chapter 12

The next morning, Jack and I were eating breakfast when my phone rang; it was Kathy. I'd tried to contact her a few times over the weekend to find out how Grandma had reacted to her resignation, but I hadn't been able to get hold of her.

"Jill. I thought I ought to ring because I've got a million missed calls from you."

"I was beginning to think you'd been abducted by aliens."

"Pete decided we should have a weekend away to celebrate my leaving Ever. We went down to London."

"I didn't realise they don't have network coverage down there."

"Sorry. Pete thought it would be a good idea to switch off our phones, so there'd be no distractions."

"What about the kids?"

"We took them with us. We all went to see Aladdin — they loved it."

"It's alright for some. I spent most of yesterday rescuing vegetables."

"Doing what?"

"I'll explain another time. What happened with Grandma? How many shades of red did she turn when you told her you were leaving?"

"She didn't. She said she'd be sorry to lose me, and wished me well."

"No, seriously. What did she really say?"

"Honestly, that was it. She couldn't have been any nicer about it."

"Did she ask what you were going to be doing?"

"Yeah. She seemed genuinely interested in my plans for the shop."

"You're sure it was Grandma you spoke to?"

"She was really sweet, Jill. Maybe you and I have misjudged her."

Somehow, I doubted that.

"I wonder how the vegetables are doing next door," Jack said when I'd finished on the call. "I haven't heard any shouting."

"Maybe Clare has killed him. I'd definitely kill you if you were cheating on me with a runner bean."

"What if I cheated with a courgette?"

"That'd be okay, but I'll have no truck with beans."

"By the way, how are the wedding plans coming along?"

"What?" I almost choked on my cornflakes.

"Mrs V's wedding plans? Have there been any more developments?"

I shrugged. "I'm trying not to get too involved."

"Why not? I love weddings."

"Is that the time? I'd better be making tracks."

Before I could, my phone rang again; this time it was Aunt Lucy.

"I'm sorry to call you so early, Jill."

"That's okay. Is everything alright?"

"Yes. At least I think so, but the strangest thing just happened."

Jack gestured to me that he was leaving, and blew me a kiss.

Aunt Lucy continued, "I've just told your grandmother that we're going to be moving to a new house."

"Oh dear. How did that go, as if I didn't know?"

"That's just it. She said she was pleased for us."

"No way."

"Yes, and what's more, she sounded like she meant it. I kept waiting for the snide remark, but she couldn't have been any nicer."

"She must be ill."

"That's a little uncharitable."

"Something's definitely not right. Kathy handed her notice in at Ever on Friday, and Grandma said she was sorry to lose her, and wished her well. You're not telling me that this is normal behaviour for Grandma. She's definitely up to something."

"Maybe, but for now, I'm prepared to give her the benefit of the doubt. I'm going to Cuppy C later. Do you fancy joining me?"

"Why not? We can try to figure out who's taken over Grandma's body. Give me a call when you're there."

***

Jules was at her desk, knitting.

"Morning, Jules. I haven't seen you knitting for a while."

"I said I'd make Dexter a jumper."

"I take it you two are okay now, then?"

"Yeah. He still keeps apologising for leaving me stranded, even though I've told him it's okay. I visited his grandma in hospital; she's a darling."

"How is she doing?"

"She seems to have bounced back remarkably well; she's already back home. I told Dexter I'd like to go and see her again."

Oh bum!

"Maybe it would be best to give her some time to recover."

"That's what Dexter said. He's got himself really worked up over all of this. He even got his own grandmother's name mixed up."

Winky was on *my* desk, on *my* computer.

"Excuse me," I said. "Just whose office do you think this is?"

"Mine, of course, but you're welcome to use it from time to time."

I looked over his shoulder, and saw a screen full of figures. "What's that you're looking at?"

"It's my investment portfolio."

"You're always telling me that you don't have any money."

"I don't have any *liquid* funds. It's all tied up in these investments."

"How much do you have altogether?"

"Never you mind." He put his paws over the screen so I couldn't see. "What about you? How much do *you* have invested?"

"Me? I — err — "

"You do have savings, I assume?"

"Yeah, of course."

"Which do you favour? Long-term, high yield bonds or the more speculative funds?"

"I — err — why do you want to know?"

"I could give you the benefit of my years of experience."

"I'm okay, thanks. When I need financial advice from a

cat, I'll know I'm in real trouble."

"Please yourself. Don't say I didn't offer."

Bonds? Funds? I had no clue what he was talking about. The precious little savings I had were in my bank account, or in the piggy bank I kept hidden in the spare bedroom.

What? Of course I needed to hide it. If Jack got his hands on it, he'd probably buy yet another bowling shirt.

***

I didn't bother to kick Winky off the computer because I'd arranged to meet with Thomas Bradley's PA, Ruth Foot.

Lucas Broad was behind the reception desk when I arrived at the Nexler Building.

"Hi again. I'm here to see Ruth Foot."

"She said you were coming. She's over there, in the meeting room where you and I spoke the other day."

"Great. Thanks. Did you bring that DVD in?"

"Sorry. I meant to, but I was in such a rush this morning that I forgot all about it. I'll bring it in tomorrow."

"Okay. No problem."

"I hope this is okay." Ruth had organised tea for us both. "I can get someone to bring coffee if you'd prefer it?"

"Tea's fine, thanks."

"I thought it made sense to talk in here, so we don't get interrupted by the phone."

"That's fine. I assume the fact that you're still at West Star after all this time, means you've been happy here?"

"Yes, I have. Because I've been here from the very

beginning, I feel like I'm a part of the business rather than just an employee."

"I believe you were the one who found Stephen's body?"

The question seemed to knock the wind out of her, and it took her a few moments to respond. "I still have nightmares about that day."

"That's understandable. I'm sorry to have to put you through this."

"It's okay. Back then, I was responsible for everything, including the washing up. Typical men—neither Thomas nor Stephen would ever think to wash their cups. I used to do them first thing every morning before the guys arrived. I didn't see him at first—not until I went behind the desk to get his cup." She hesitated again. "The carpet was stained with blood, and I knew straight away he was dead."

"Were you the one who rang the police?"

"I actually rang Thomas first. I don't know why; I guess I wasn't thinking straight. He told me to call the police. The rest of that day is still a blur."

"What was Stephen like, as a person and as an employer?"

"He was a lovely man, and a great boss. Always very considerate."

"What time did you leave on the night of the murder?"

"About eight o'clock. I tried never to work later than that."

"And both Thomas and Stephen were still here then?"

"That's right."

"I believe that the cleaner normally came in late at night?"

"Yes, if memory serves, she used to come in at about eleven o'clock."

"Isn't that rather late?"

"Yeah, it is. West Star didn't have much money back then, but we managed to get a cheap deal from a woman who had just set up her own cleaning business. She was still working a full-time job in the daytime, and then she ran the cleaning business in the evenings. I don't know how she managed it. If she had come in that night, she would have been the one to find Stephen."

"Why didn't she come in?"

"I'm not sure. Maybe she was ill. I know the police spoke to her."

"How was the brothers' relationship just prior to Stephen's death?"

"It wasn't great."

"Why do you say that? Was it because of the disagreement about the potential takeover?"

"That didn't help, but it wasn't the only issue. Did you know that Thomas was seeing Georgina before Stephen's death?"

"Yes, she told me."

"But did you know that Stephen knew about their affair?"

"Are you sure? Georgina and Thomas don't think he did."

"I know for certain that he knew about it because he told me."

"When did he tell you?"

"The day he was murdered. He said he was going to have it out with Thomas."

"Did he?"

"Not while I was there, but they were both still in the office when I left."

"Did you tell the police about this?"

She shook her head.

"Why not?"

"If I had, it would have looked bad for Thomas, and I was sure he wasn't the one who killed Stephen. I hope I was right to do that."

"What do you mean?"

"Thomas does have a temper." She hesitated. "But he would never have hurt Stephen."

What a bombshell!

It turned out that Stephen did know about the affair, and he'd intended confronting his brother that night. Although Ruth Foot had covered for Thomas at the time, she'd admitted he did have a temper. It wasn't too much of a stretch to believe that things could have escalated and become physical. That would point to Thomas as the murderer, but there was one flaw with that theory: the CCTV evidence that showed Thomas had left before Stephen was murdered.

***

I was on my way back to the office when Aunt Lucy called to say she was just about to go to Cuppy C. I magicked myself over there, and found both Amber and Pearl behind the counter.

"Jill, I want to ask you a favour," Amber said, before we even had a chance to place our order.

"I should get to ask first," Pearl objected.

"Too late. I got in first."

"Girls, enough. What are you both going on about?"

"Will you ask your PA if she'll knit some baby clothes for Lil or Phil?" Amber said.

"But not until she's knitted some for Lil or Bill." Pearl scowled at her sister.

"I thought you two weren't going to tell each other the names you'd chosen?"

"*We* didn't." Pearl glared at Aunt Lucy. "*Someone else* did."

"I'm not keeping your secrets," Aunt Lucy said. "And besides, it's just as well I did tell you because at least now you know you've come up with the same name for a girl. One of you will have to have a rethink."

"If you both have a girl, one of you could call her Jill," I suggested.

The twins looked at me, and said in perfect harmony, "Nah."

"What's wrong with Jill?"

"Nothing's wrong with it," Pearl said. "I just prefer Lil."

"William and I came up with Lil first." Amber glared at her sister.

"No, you didn't. Alan and I did, and we're not changing it."

"Neither are we."

"Come on, you two." Aunt Lucy stepped in. "You have to be sensible. If you both have girls, they can't both be called Lil."

"She'd better come up with another name, then." Amber pointed at her sister.

"No chance. You'll have to change yours."

The argument was set to run and run, so Aunt Lucy and I collared one of the other assistants to take our order.

"You've started something there," I said, once we were seated by the window.

"I had to say something. Fool that I am, I assumed one of them would be happy to go for another name."

"You really don't know your own daughters, do you?"

"Apparently not. And it seems that neither you nor I know your grandmother as well as we thought we did."

"She's up to something."

"You're not being very fair, Jill."

"Come on. Do you honestly believe she's changed?"

"Stranger things have happened."

"Name one."

"Okay, I agree that it's totally out of character, but I for one am glad for her new persona, even if it's only short lived."

Just then, the strangest thing happened: Our cups and plates slid off the table and dropped to the floor. The same thing happened on every other table. Even weirder was the fact that none of the cups or plates smashed. Instead they seemed to bounce.

"What's going on?" Aunt Lucy began to sway back and forth on her chair.

I was swaying too; so was everyone else.

The reason for these unusual happenings soon became apparent. The furniture and the floor had all changed texture. It was as if everything was made from rubber.

The other customers began to panic, and started to head for the door, which wasn't easy because their feet sank into the floor with every step. Eventually, the only people left in the shop were me, Aunt Lucy and the twins.

"We thought of Lil first!" Amber yelled.

"No, you didn't. We did!" Pearl shouted back.

Unbelievable! They were still arguing about baby names, and hadn't even noticed what had happened.

"Hey! You two!" I shouted.

"Where is everyone?" Pearl glanced around.

"Why are all the pots on the floor?" Amber said.

"Look." I pushed the table, which wobbled back and forth.

"What's happened?" Pearl looked horrified.

"The floor's the same." Amber took a few unsteady steps out from behind the counter.

"This must be magic of some kind," Aunt Lucy said. "It looks very like the 'softer' spell, but it can't be because I've just tried to reverse it, and nothing happened. Why don't you try, Jill?"

I did, but it had no effect.

"Why would someone do this to us?" Pearl said.

"We need to find your grandmother." Aunt Lucy began to walk rather unsteadily towards the door. "She'll know what to do."

Pearl and Amber had forgotten their squabble, and both now looked very worried.

"It's going to be alright." I made my way slowly over to the wobbly counter.

"What if it's not?" Pearl was close to tears. "This shop is our livelihood."

"It'll be okay, Pearl." Amber put her arm around her sister.

It never failed to amaze me how one minute they could

be at each other's throat, and then the next, they had each other's back.

A few minutes later, Aunt Lucy returned with Grandma by her side.

"Grandma, you have to help us," Amber said.

Grandma quickly barked out her orders, "You all need to get out of here right now."

"But Grandma—" Pearl began.

"I said get out. Now!"

"Do you want me to stay?" I asked.

"Which part of *all of you* don't you understand?"

Aunt Lucy, the twins and I made our way out of the shop. All we could do now was watch and wait.

Chapter 13

It was obvious that Grandma was trying to reverse the spell, but it was equally obvious that she was having zero success because the furniture was still wobbling back and forth. Eventually, she gave up and walked unsteadily to the door.

"Jill, get in here!"

"Can you sort it out, Grandma?" Amber shouted.

Grandma didn't even acknowledge her question; she just waited until I was inside, and then closed the door.

"Lucy was right. This is the 'softer' spell."

"I saw you trying to reverse it."

"It should have worked. I don't understand why it didn't. I've brought you in here, so we can mount a co-ordinated effort. Between us, we'll have more than enough power. Are you ready?"

"Yeah, just say the word."

"On three. One, two, three."

We both applied maximum focus, but still the spell refused to be reversed.

"What's going on, Grandma? I've never come across a spell that I couldn't reverse before. At least not for a long time."

"That makes two of us. I can't begin to imagine who could have cast a spell that would resist our combined power."

"What are we going to do?"

"First, we have to get the spell reversed, and then we need to find out who or what is behind it."

"What's the plan?"

"I'll get in touch with a few level six witches who owe

me a favour. We'll all meet here tomorrow morning. Let's say ten-thirty."

"I'll be here. What are you going to tell the twins?"

"*I'm* not going to tell them anything—that's your job. I have a lot of phone calls to make."

Grandma led the way out of Cuppy C, leaving me to face the twins.

"What's happening, Jill?" Pearl asked.

"Grandma's going to recruit some more level six witches, so we can try again to reverse the spell tomorrow morning."

"What if it doesn't work?" Amber looked worried.

"It will. No spell will be able to resist the power of several level six witches."

"What shall we do now?"

"You might as well lock up the shop and go home. There's nothing else you can do."

The twins had no sooner left than my phone rang. It was the photographer who worked with the Pooch First Model Agency. He'd had a cancellation and wondered if there was any chance that I could take Barry for his photoshoot in an hour's time. The sooner Barry was on the agency's books, the sooner he would start earning his keep, so I told them we'd be there.

"I take it that was about Barry?" Aunt Lucy said, after I'd finished on the call.

"Yeah. I'll walk back with you, and then take Barry over to the photographer's."

"Do you really think that all of you will be able to reverse the 'softer' spell tomorrow, or were you just saying that to stop the twins from worrying?"

"To be perfectly honest, I don't know what will happen. By rights, Grandma and I should have been able to reverse the spell easily. Whoever cast it must be extremely powerful."

"Who could be powerful enough to do something like this?"

"I don't know. Unless — no, it couldn't be."

"What were you going to say, Jill?"

"From what I've heard, Braxmore had incredible powers."

"Do you think it might be him?"

"I'm not sure. No one is even sure if he's still alive. But right now, I'm struggling to come up with any other explanation."

***

"Jill! Can we go for a walk?" Barry came charging over, and almost knocked me flat. "I love to go for walks."

"Not now."

"Aww, please."

"You have to have your photos taken for the modelling agency."

"Take my photos? Right now?"

"Yeah, they've had a cancellation."

"Do I look good, Jill?"

"You look as handsome as ever."

"Give me strength," Hamlet said, without even looking up from his book.

Barry ran across to the cage. "I'm going to be a supermodel, Hamlet."

"I'm very pleased for you, I'm sure. Now, if you

wouldn't mind, Dickens awaits."

"Come on, Barry. We'd better be making tracks." I put on his lead, and he practically dragged me all the way across town to the photographer's studio, which turned out to be above a millinery shop called Top Hats. If only Mrs V had been able to travel to Candlefield, she would definitely have approved.

The studio was called Len's Lens. Len, the photographer, was a pleasant middle-aged wizard with a penchant for tartan.

"This must be Barry. I've heard good things about you, boy."

"I'm going to be a supermodel," Barry barked out.

"Confidence is no bad thing in this line of work. Still, first things first. Let's take some photographs for your portfolio." Len turned to me. "I find it works best if the owners wait in reception while I take the photos. It's one less thing to distract him. Would you mind?"

"Not at all."

Barry happily followed Len into the studio while I helped myself to a drink, of what tasted like dishwater, from the vending machine. Hanging around in reception gave me the chance to mull over the 'floppy' issue at Cuppy C. I was much more worried than I'd let on to Aunt Lucy. Only an extremely powerful wizard or witch could have cast a spell so strong that the combined efforts of Grandma and I couldn't reverse it. I knew of no such witch, but from what I'd heard, Braxmore might have been powerful enough to do it. But why would he waste his time on an attack on Cuppy C?

Just then, my phone rang.

"Jill. It's Harry from Spooky Wooky."

"Hi, Harry."

"I'm calling because we wanted to thank you for helping with the Spookberry potion."

"Has the colonel been to see you?"

"Yes. He and Priscilla were in here just now. He's going to let us have some Spookberry so we can attend the grand opening of the bakery."

"That's great news."

"Thanks again for your help, Jill. The blueberry muffins are on us for the rest of the month."

"That really isn't necessary, *but* if you insist."

Free muffins for a month — what a result! Now I needed to fulfil my part of the bargain with the colonel, by putting Homer Range out of business. I'd had an idea how to do it, but I would need to speak to Constance Bowler before I could put my plan into action.

"All done." Len appeared with Barry by his side.

"How did it go?" I asked. "Did he behave himself?"

"He was as good as gold. Would you like to see the shots?"

"Yes, please."

Barry was incredibly photogenic. The big, soft lummox looked almost regal in the pictures Len had taken.

"He should do very well," Len said.

"Do you really think so?"

"Definitely. I see a lot of dogs, as you can imagine. Barry is one of the best."

"Did you hear that, Jill?" Barry's tail was going ten to the dozen. "I'm one of the best!"

"I did. Well done you." I turned to Len. "What happens now?"

"I'll get the photos over to Pooch First, and they'll no doubt get the ball rolling. I doubt he'll be waiting long for his first assignment."

***

By the time I'd dropped Barry back at Aunt Lucy's, I was feeling a little peckish. What better way to satisfy my hunger than with a blueberry muffin? And better still: a free one.

I magicked myself over to Spooky Wooky in GT.

Harry and Larry were both behind the counter. Larry in particular looked pleased to see me. He turned to Harry, "I win, I believe."

Harry shook his head, took out his wallet, and handed over a couple of bank notes.

"Thanks for this, Jill." Larry waved the cash.

"What do you mean?"

"We had a wager on how long it would take you to claim your first free muffin. I said you'd be in within a couple of hours. Harry said it would take you at least four."

"What if I hadn't shown up for a week?"

For some reason, they both laughed at that.

I'd no sooner taken a seat than Constance Bowler walked in.

"Constance! Could I have a word?"

"Sure. I'll be with you as soon as I've got my drink."

"Is that all you're having?" I said when she joined me.

"Yeah, I just needed a coffee. I try not to eat between meals."

"Me too."

She glanced at the muffin, and raised her eyebrows.

"I thought I'd make an exception today."

"Right. Do you make many exceptions?"

"Not many. Anyway, I'm glad I've caught you. I wanted to talk to you about the Spookberry situation."

"Did you manage to sort anything out for Harry and Larry?"

"Yes. The colonel came through for me, but he's asked a favour in return. His business is being badly hit by a black marketeer by the name of Homer Range, so I've promised to see what I can do about it. He tells me that the police won't get involved with licensing issues. Is that right?"

"He's right and wrong. We don't have the resources to check that everyone using Spookberry has a licence, but that doesn't mean we'll turn a blind eye to anyone peddling it on an industrial scale."

"That's reassuring because I'm planning to go after Homer Range, but there's little point in my doing that unless you're prepared to take action against him."

"If you can get proof that he's selling large quantities of Spookberry, then we'll arrest him."

"That's great. In that case, expect a call from me in the not too distant future."

Constance and I chatted for almost half-an-hour before she was called away. It was only then that I spotted Blodwyn and Alberto seated at the back of the tea room. They must have come in while I was deep in conversation.

"Hello, you two."

"Hi, Jill." Blodwyn looked as though she'd just finished sucking on a lemon.

"Hello, Jill." Alberto didn't look much happier. "We didn't come and join you earlier because we could see you were talking."

"Where's Mum and Dad?"

"No idea." Blodwyn shook her head.

"Darlene's back at the house," Alberto said.

"Is everything okay? You two don't look very happy."

"Is there any wonder?" Blodwyn snapped. "Those parents of yours are making both of our lives a misery."

"Take no notice of us," Alberto said. "We're just crying on one another's shoulders."

"What exactly have my parents done?"

"You've seen what they're like," Blodwyn said. "They're at each other's throats all the time. It's driving me and Alberto crazy."

"Have either of you confronted them?"

"I've tried to," Alberto said. "But you know what your mother is like. She's not known for her listening skills."

"Josh is even worse. It's like talking to a brick wall." Blodwyn hesitated. "I tell you, Jill. If things don't change soon, I'm off."

"The way they're acting is beyond ridiculous," I said. "Those two are as bad as one another. Do you mind if I make a suggestion?"

"Knock yourself out." Blodwyn shrugged. "We're all out of ideas."

"Why don't you let me speak to them both."

"I'm not sure it will do any good," Alberto said.

"I'd like to try. With your permission."

They both nodded their agreement.

As soon as I'd left the tea room, I made a call to

Constance Bowler.

"Jill? When you said you'd call, I didn't think you meant quite so soon."

"This isn't about the Spookberry. I'm hoping you might be able to recommend a restaurant here in GT. I need somewhere a little upmarket."

"Are you celebrating something?"

"Not exactly. It needs to be somewhere you have to be on your best behaviour. Somewhere they won't tolerate raised voices or unseemly behaviour."

"Poltergeist Nouveau sounds like the kind of place you're looking for. It's quite expensive, but worth every penny. They won't put up with any nonsense that might upset their other customers."

"That sounds just the ticket. Thanks, Constance."

***

When I arrived home, Clare was taking her grocery shopping into the house. I hoped I might avoid her, but she spotted me, and came over.

"I just wanted to apologise for yesterday, Jill."

"There's no need."

"Yes, there is. I should have waited until we were back home before laying into Tony like that."

"How are things now?"

"Not good. I take it you realised that the runner bean was an old flame of Tony's."

"Yeah. I assumed so."

"He still denies that he arranged to meet her, but I'm not sure I believe him."

"Where is he now?"

"I haven't thrown him out if that's what you mean. He's at work. I don't want to do anything rash."

"Very sensible. Do you have any more cons planned?"

"We've got one on Saturday." She rolled her eyes. "It's CupidCon."

"Oh dear."

I was just about to go into the house when I glanced across the street, and noticed that the balaclava twins' van wasn't on their drive. This was my chance to see if I could find anything which might confirm my suspicion that they were in fact the witchfinders, Vinnie and Minnie Dreadmore.

I made my way casually across the road, and when I was sure there was no one looking, I slipped around the back of their house. There, in the back garden, were all the buckets that the balaclava twins had purchased from the corner shop. What on earth were they doing with them?

"Can I help you?" The woman's voice made me jump.

I spun around to find the female half of the balaclava twins standing in her back doorway.

"Oh? Hi. I—err—I've just been to the corner shop. I was hoping to buy a bucket, but Jack Corner told me that you'd bought all of his stock."

"So?"

"I wondered if you'd be willing to sell me one?" I glanced at the huge pile of buckets. "If you have any to spare, that is."

"No, sorry. We need them all."

"You do have rather a lot of them. I'd only need the one."

"We don't have any to spare. Sorry. Was there anything

else?"

"Did you enjoy the cake we brought you?"

"We threw it away. We don't eat dairy or gluten."

"Right. Okay, well, I'd better be off then. Nice to see—"

She'd already slammed the door closed.

Chapter 14

The next morning, I waited until Jack had left for work, and then made a call to my mother in Ghost Town.

"Jill? Is everything okay?"

"Yeah. It just occurred to me that we haven't seen much of each other recently."

"That's partly my fault. I've been tied up with Alberto's stupid garden tours until recently."

"I thought it would be nice for us to go out for dinner."

"That's a great idea. It's a while since Alberto and I—"

"Actually, I was hoping that just the two of us could have a night out. We never really get the chance to talk properly. It would be an opportunity for us to catch up."

"That would be lovely. When did you have in mind?"

"I realise it's short notice, but I've taken the liberty of booking a table tonight at Poltergeist Nouveau. I hope that's okay?"

"Err—yes, that's fine. I've never been there, but I hear it's very nice. Very expensive too."

"That doesn't matter. It will be my treat. Is eight o'clock okay?"

"Eight's fine. I look forward to it."

"Great. I'll see you there, then."

One down. One to go.

"Dad, it's me."

"Hi, Jill. How lovely to hear your voice. I was only saying to Blodwyn yesterday that I hadn't seen you for a while."

"I wondered if you'd like to get dinner with me tonight? Just the two of us?"

"Tonight? Sure, I'd love to. What's the occasion?"

"There doesn't need to be an occasion, does there?"

"Of course not."

"I've booked a table at Poltergeist Nouveau for ten past eight. I hope that works for you."

"That'll be fine. You must let me pay, though. I hear that place is rather expensive."

"I wouldn't hear of it. This will be my treat. I'll see you there tonight."

***

When I arrived at the office building, there was a queue of women stretching halfway down the stairs. As I made my way past them, a woman with pink hair grabbed me by the arm.

"Hey! Get in the queue."

"I'm not going to the nail bar. My office is just there at the top of the stairs."

"Oh, sorry."

"Are they still running special offers? I thought that was just the first two days?"

"Nah. The offers have finished. Everyone's here for Nails."

"Yeah, I gathered that." I grinned. "It is a nail bar after all."

She shook her head. "I don't mean that. I'm mean the guy who works there. Everyone calls him Nails. He's the best nail technician in the country. That's what I heard, anyway."

"*Really*? Are you sure about that?"

"Yeah. It's all over Instagram. My cousin got hers done

here yesterday, and they're mint. Never seen anything like it."

Nails a superstar? Who would have thought it?

"Morning, Mrs V."

"Morning, Jill. What do you think about pageboys?"

"To be honest, I've never given them much thought."

"I have two great-nieces: Sandy and Mandy. They both have young sons. Sandy's little boy is called Andy. Mandy's boy is called — err — now what is it? It's on the tip of my tongue. It starts with 'R'."

"Randy?"

"No. Raymond, that's it. Anyway, when I mentioned to Sandy that Armi and I were getting married, she asked if Andy could be a pageboy, and I said yes. But then, when I told Mandy about the wedding, she said that Raymond wanted to be a pageboy, too."

"What's the problem? Can't you just have two pageboys?"

"Normally, I'd say yes, but Andy and Raymond have never got along. Whenever they're in the same room, they end up fighting."

"Oh dear."

"I never realised that planning a wedding would be so difficult. You've got all this to come, Jill."

"Not for a very long time."

"That's not the impression Kathy gave me."

"Kathy? When did you see her? What's she been saying?"

"I bumped into her on the High Street yesterday. She was telling me all about her plans for Kathy's Bridal Shop. She said that you and Jack had been discussing your future, and that he was expected to pop the question any day now."

"That's nonsense. Jack and I have never discussed getting married. Kathy must have got the wrong end of the stick as usual."

"Pity. We could have had a double wedding. Just think how much we could both save."

"Sorry, Mrs V, but that's not going to happen. Anyway, I must get on."

"What about the pageboys? What do you think I should do about them?"

"Buy them both a pair of boxing gloves?"

"I have the perfect solution," Winky said as soon as I walked into my office.

"To what?"

"The old bag lady's pageboy conundrum."

"Have you been *tabby* hanging again."

"Was that supposed to be funny?" He rolled his eye.

"Apparently not. Anyway, you shouldn't be listening to our conversations. They're private."

"Don't you want to hear my solution to the pageboy problem?"

"Not really."

"She should forget about Andy and Randy."

"Raymond."

"Whatever. She should dump that idea, and have a pagecat instead."

"That's very funny." I laughed.

"I'm not joking. I'd be great at it. I'd look good in a tux."

"Mrs V isn't going to agree to having you as her pageboy."

"Pagecat."

"It's never going to happen."

"You could at least float the idea to her."

"No chance. She already thinks I've got a few slates loose."

Just then, the temperature dropped, and realising that a ghost was about to materialise, Winky shot under the sofa.

"Hi, Colonel."

"Sorry to drop in unannounced, Jill. I hope I'm not interrupting anything important."

"It's fine. I was just talking to my cat."

"I haven't seen that one-eyed terror for a while." He glanced around. "Where's he hiding?"

"He's under there. He isn't very fond of ghosts, I'm afraid."

"Of course. I sometimes forget that I'm a ghost." He crouched down, so he could see under the sofa. "Come on, boy. I won't hurt you."

Winky didn't budge; he just hissed at the colonel.

"I popped in to let you know that I've sorted Harry and Larry out with the Spookberry."

"So I understand."

"Have you had any thoughts on that scoundrel, Homer Range?"

"I have as it happens, but to put my plan into action, I'm going to need the use of your old house again. Do you think there's any chance of that?"

"As luck would have it, Murray Murray has just embarked on a European tour. He's going to be away for two months. You can use the house any time that suits you. What did you have in mind?"

"I've spoken to Constance Bowler. She confirmed that the police will take action against Range if I can provide her with proof that he's selling unlicensed Spookberry in quantity. I plan to do just that."

"Excellent. The sooner that blaggard is behind bars, the better. Is there anything I can do to help?"

"It would make life easier if you could be at the house to let me in."

"When?"

"I'm not sure yet. I'll let you know once I have everything organised."

"Right you are, Jill. I'd better be getting back. I promised I'd take Priscilla shopping for a new dress." He crouched down again. "Bye, Winky old boy."

Winky hissed even louder.

***

When I arrived at Cuppy C, the twins and Aunt Lucy were standing outside. Grandma was already in the shop, along with another twelve witches, most of whom I recognised from the various competitions I'd taken part in.

"Do you think it will work this time, Jill?" Amber asked, anxiously.

"Yeah, I'm sure it will."

What else was I going to say? In truth, I was feeling far from confident.

"You're the last one to arrive as usual." Grandma greeted me when I walked through the door.

"You said ten-thirty. It's only—"

"Never mind that. We have work to do." She turned to the other witches, and called for order. "You all know why we're here. It's pretty obvious which spell we're up against, so if we all focus on reversing the 'softer' spell, I see no reason why it shouldn't work. Does anyone have any questions?"

There were none.

"Good. In that case, we'll go on three. One, two, three."

I'd never experienced anything quite like the combined force of so many witches. Everyone had their eyes closed to ensure maximum focus on the task in hand. When I eventually opened mine, the floor and tables were as wobbly as before.

No one spoke for the longest moment, but then Grandma broke the silence.

"I've never seen anything like this. No spell should be able to withstand our combined power."

"Is this Braxmore's work?" Katrina Corke asked.

"I don't know, but we can't dismiss that possibility. Whoever cast this spell has the power equivalent to more than a dozen level six witches."

"How many witches do you think it would take to break the spell, Mirabel?" A witch I didn't recognise asked.

"How am I supposed to know that, Deirdre?" Grandma snapped.

While Grandma continued to respond to questions, I started for the door.

"Where do you think you're going?" She called after me.

"I thought I'd better tell the twins what had happened."

"I'm sure they can see for themselves."

"Would you rather I stayed?"

"No, you may as well go. There's nothing more to be done for the moment. I'll need to give this some more thought. Make sure you all keep your phones close by because I may need to call you back here at short notice."

I'd lied when I'd told Grandma my reason for leaving was to update the twins. As she'd pointed out, they didn't need to be told that our attempts to reverse the spell had failed; that was obvious for anyone to see. I had another reason for wanting to get away.

After magicking myself back to Washbridge, I made a phone call.

"Alicia. It's Jill. Can you tell me which unit on the industrial estate Ma Chivers has those witches working out of?"

"Why? What are you planning to do?"

"Pay it a visit."

"That could be dangerous."

"I'm prepared to take that risk."

"At least let me come with you."

"No. Just tell me which unit they're in."

"Thirty-one."

"Okay. Thanks."

At this point, the sensible thing to do would have been to tell Grandma what I was planning. But no one could ever accuse me of being sensible. And besides, this long shot was *so long* that I didn't want to make myself look a complete fool in front of her.

What? Yes, I do know what comes before a fall. Thanks for the reminder, though.

I could have simply magicked myself to the Flawton Industrial Estate, but I opted to drive there. That way, I figured I would give myself enough time to formulate a carefully constructed plan of action.

At least, that was the theory, but when I arrived there, I still had zero idea of what I was going to do.

Unit thirty-one was at the far side of the small industrial estate. The single-storey building was nondescript; it didn't even have a sign to indicate the nature of the business inside.

I made my way to reception, but the door was locked, and I couldn't see anyone through the window. I tried the bell but there was no response. Had Alicia sent me on some kind of wild goose chase?

I cast the 'listen' spell. If there were dozens of witches working inside, then I should be able to hear them.

There was only silence.

Thank goodness I hadn't dragged Grandma here; she would have given me so much grief.

"Achoo!"

The sound of someone sneezing stopped me dead in my tracks. I waited several minutes, but heard no more sounds. I was just on the point of abandoning this fool's errand when I heard another sneeze. There was definitely someone inside, and I needed to find out what they were up to.

The 'power' spell made short work of the fire door at the back of the building. Once inside, I listened again, but could hear nothing. After walking by a number of empty offices, I came upon a set of rubber doors. I pushed them aside, walked into the large room, and then stared in disbelief at the sight that greeted me.

Seated at row upon row of tables were at least a hundred witches. On each table was a tiny cube, little bigger than a dice. The witches didn't appear to register my arrival, and although they were all sitting upright, they had their eyes closed as though they were asleep. None of them stirred as I walked up and down the aisles.

I had no idea what was going on.

"Excuse me," I said to the witch seated at the end of one of the rows.

She didn't react.

"Excuse me!" Louder this time. When that didn't work, I gave her a gentle shake.

"What?" Her eyes blinked open. "Who are you?"

"Never mind that. What are you doing?"

"What do you mean?"

"You seemed to be in some kind of trance."

"I was casting a spell. The same one, over and over."

"Which spell?"

"Why? Who are you? Do you work for Ma Chivers?"

"No. Look, this is very important. Which spell were you casting?"

"The 'softer' spell."

"But what were you casting it on? There's nothing here—apart from this tiny little box? What is that anyway?"

"It's a spell battery."

"What does it do?"

"Ma Chivers sells them to companies in the human world that need to soften their products."

"That's nonsense."

"It's what she told us. Why else would she be paying us to work on them?"

"I don't care what she told you. Your magic is being used for evil purposes in Candlefield."

"That can't be right."

"It most certainly is. Do you know Cuppy C?"

"The twins' tea room?"

"That's right. The twins are my cousins."

"Are you Jill Gooder?"

"Yes."

"Sorry, Jill, I didn't recognise you. I'm still feeling a little out of it. I've never focussed on a single spell for such a long time. What were you saying about Cuppy C?"

"It's been put out of action. Someone has cast the 'softer' spell on the furniture and floor."

"Couldn't it have been cast by a level six witch who the twins had upset? They can be a little offhanded sometimes."

"No, it's not that. Earlier today, a dozen level six witches tried to reverse the spell, and we couldn't."

"Wow!"

"Exactly. Somehow, Ma Chivers is using these so-called batteries to power a spell so powerful it's practically impossible to reverse."

"That's terrible. I wouldn't have had anything to do with it if I'd known. I doubt any of the others would have either. Is there anything I can do to help?"

"Is Ma Chivers anywhere around?"

"I'm not sure, but I doubt it. She usually comes in at the beginning of the day, and then again just before we leave."

"Good. In that case, you can help me to snap all the others out of their focus, and then I'll explain what's going on to everyone."

It took us almost an hour to bring all of the witches out of their trance-like state.

"Ladies. Can I have your attention, please? There's something important that you all need to know. The 'work' that Ma Chivers has you doing is not what it seems."

"Where is Ma Chivers?" A witch in the back row shouted. "Who are you, anyway?"

"Are you stupid?" Someone from the row in front of her turned around. "That's Jill Gooder."

"Oh, right. Sorry, I didn't realise."

I continued, "Ma Chivers isn't selling these *batteries* to businesses in the human world. I believe that she's using their combined power for evil in Candlefield."

"What do you mean by *evil*? What is she doing with them?"

"As we speak, my cousins' tea room, Cuppy C, has been put out of action with a 'softer' spell that we've been unable to reverse. I'm ninety-nine percent certain that it's being powered by your spells."

"That's terrible."

"I can't believe she'd do something like that. Are you sure, Jill?"

"As sure as I can be. That's why I'm going to ask you to stop what you're doing, and leave with me."

"What about the money we're owed?" a witch on the front row said.

"I'm sorry to say I don't think you're ever going to see that."

"I was relying on that money."

"Look, if any of you still want to stay after what you've just heard, I can't stop you, but do you really trust someone who is capable of doing something like this?"

Five minutes later, I led the way out of the building. No one opted to stay behind.

Chapter 15

After driving back to Washbridge, I parked the car and then magicked myself to Cuppy C. The twins were inside the shop, looking very sorry for themselves.

I walked unsteadily across the wobbly floor to the wobbly counter.

"Where's Grandma?"

"She's gone," Amber said. "They've all gone."

"If all those level six witches and you can't help us, we're doomed." Pearl looked close to tears.

"Don't be silly. It's much too soon to give up."

"That's easy for you to say, Jill," Amber snapped. "You're not the one whose business is going down the drain."

"We're going to sort this out, I promise."

"How?"

"I'm almost certain Ma Chivers is behind this."

"Ma Chivers?" Pearl scoffed. "How can it be her? She isn't powerful enough to do something like this."

"Alicia told me that Ma Chivers has been recruiting witches to work in the human world, and—"

"Since when did you trust anything Alicia said?" Amber interrupted.

"Never mind that. I've just come back from a factory in Washbridge where Ma Chivers had more than a hundred witches all casting the same spell. Guess which one?"

"The 'softer' spell?" Pearl said.

"Bingo!"

"How could what they're doing in the human world affect Cuppy C?"

"Ma Chivers seems to have developed some kind of

battery that is able to 'store' the spell."

"And you think she's used the 'batteries' to do this?" Amber gestured around the shop.

"I think so, but it would take an awful lot of them to have this kind of effect."

"But we'd know if she'd planted lots of batteries in here, wouldn't we?"

"Each one is very small; no bigger than a dice. To have had this kind of effect, she would have had to plant lots of them."

"She hasn't been in here for ages, though."

"What are you three doing in here?" Grandma came through the door, and wobbled her way over to join us.

"Jill thinks she knows what's behind this," Amber said.

"Oh?" Grandma turned to me. "And were you thinking of telling me anytime soon?"

"I've only just got back from Washbridge. I didn't want to say anything until—"

"Stop waffling, woman, and spit it out."

I told Grandma about Ma Chivers' factory and the spell batteries. Surprisingly, she listened and didn't interrupt even once. When I'd finished, I fully expected her to tell me that my theory was stupid, but she said, "I think you're right."

"Sorry?" I couldn't possibly have heard her correctly.

"I said you're right. It's the only thing that makes any sense. All we have to do now is find the batteries." She turned to the twins. "You two, I need you to think carefully. Who was in here in the days just before this happened?"

"But Grandma," Pearl said. "It's a tea room. There are people coming in and out all the time."

"I'm not stupid. I know that. We're looking for someone carrying something big enough to hold a large number of spell batteries. Have you had any deliveries in the last few days?"

"Only the usual cake deliveries, but we unpack those ourselves."

"Wait a minute," I said. "The other day when I was in here, that guy came to install a smart meter. He could barely carry his tool box."

"That must be it," Grandma said. "Where is the meter?"

"It's through here." Pearl led the way into the back room.

"Look!" I pointed to the dials. "They're not moving."

"That's probably because all the machines in the shop are switched off," Amber said.

"The lights are still on, so the meter should be registering something."

"What shall we do?" Pearl asked.

"We'll have to get the utility company to send someone out," Amber said.

"Stuff that." Grandma cast the 'thunderbolt' spell, which blew the meter clean off the wall, spilling dozens of tiny spell batteries onto the floor.

We carried the batteries out into the street, and then the four of us spent the next ten minutes crushing them under our feet. When we'd finished, Pearl and Amber led the charge back inside.

"Everything's back to normal!" Amber threw her arms around her sister, and the two of them cried tears of joy.

"Well done, Jill," Grandma said.

I could hardly believe my ears. "Sorry? Would you say that again?"

"Don't push your luck."

"Now I come to think of it, I thought there was something familiar about that engineer's voice. I'm pretty sure it was Ma Chivers' side-kick, Cyril. That's why he was wearing his cap pulled down over his face."

"Thank you, both." Amber gave me a hug, and then walked over to Grandma.

"Shoo!" Grandma brushed her aside. "Get away from me with your sloppy nonsense."

"What are we going to do about Ma Chivers?" I asked.

"Don't worry about her." Grandma scowled. "I'm going to undermine her."

Again, with the *undermining*. I was hoping for and expecting much worse. Was it possible that Grandma was going soft?

I was thrilled that Cuppy C was back in business for the twins' sakes. I'd never seen them quite so upset or worried about anything before.

Ma Chivers would not be a happy bunny when she discovered that her little plot had been foiled, but I didn't kid myself that would stop her for long. That woman had a seriously warped mind.

What about Alicia, though? If it hadn't been for her information, I might never have realised who was behind the plot to put Cuppy C out of business. Did that mean I should trust her now? There was still a niggling doubt in the back of my mind. What if she was playing the long game? What if the whole point of the 'softer' spell incident had been to enable Alicia to gain my confidence?

What? Just because I'm paranoid doesn't mean Alicia isn't out to get me.

One thing about the Bradley murder was still niggling at me. Why hadn't the cleaner come in that night? If she had, she would have found Stephen Bradley's body, and might even have walked in on the murderer.

I'd called Ruth Foot, but she couldn't remember the name of the cleaners that they used back then. Thomas Bradley wasn't around to ask, so on a longshot, I dropped in on the concierge, Lucas Broad.

"I don't suppose you remember the name of the company that used to clean West Star's offices at the time of Stephen Bradley's murder, do you?"

"I do as it happens." He smiled. "I had a bit of a crush on the woman who ran the company. Not that it did me any good. Her business was called Stayclean, and her name is Josey Wilde."

"Is she still in business?"

"The company definitely is. I often see the vans around Washbridge. I don't know whether she still owns it though."

"Thanks. That's very helpful."

A quick search online took me to Stayclean's website where Josey Wilde was listed as the managing director. I was about to give them a call when I noticed the address: their offices were only a five-minute walk away.

***

"Good afternoon, madam," the cheerful young man on

reception chirped. "How may I help you?"

"I'd like to see Josey Wilde, please."

"Do you have an appointment?"

"No."

"I'm afraid that without an —"

"Please tell her that it's about Stephen Bradley's murder."

"Did you say *murder*?"

"Yes. Please call her."

He didn't, but instead he disappeared through the door behind him. Either he was going to talk to his boss or he was fetching security. While I was waiting, it occurred to me that I could have picked up the DVD from Lucas Broad while I was at the Nexler. I hadn't thought about it, and Lucas hadn't mentioned it — perhaps he'd forgotten to bring it in again.

A few minutes later, the young man returned, accompanied by a smartly dressed woman in her early forties.

"I'm Josey Wilde." She offered her hand.

"Jill Gooder."

"Matthew said it was about Stephen Bradley."

"That's right. I'm a private investigator. I've been hired to look into the murder."

"After all this time?"

"Would you be prepared to answer a few questions?"

"Of course. Why don't we go through to my office?"

If her office was anything to go by, Stayclean was doing very well for itself.

"I take it that business is good?" I said.

"I can't complain. We've doubled our turnover every

year for the last three years. Mainly through acquisition."

"You've come a long way since the days when you cleaned for West Star."

"You could say that." She smiled. "Back then, I *was* Stayclean. I did everything: sales, admin and of course, the cleaning."

"And held down a full-time job from what I heard?"

"I don't know how I did it. I must have been crazy. Still, it all paid off in the end."

"I take it that your company no longer cleans for West Star?"

"No. I never cleaned for them again after the murder."

"How come?"

"I was told not to go back until further notice. I assumed it was because the offices were a crime scene, but I never heard from them again."

"Didn't you contact them?"

"I wanted to. That contract was a big deal for me back then, but it just didn't feel right to pester them. It was a major blow. I seriously considered giving it all up."

"I understand that you normally did their clean at about eleven pm? That seems very late?"

"It was, but that's because I was working full-time, and I had to run the new business around my 'real' job."

"What time did you get finished each night?"

"I started my cleaning jobs at about seven and usually finished around midnight. West Star was always my last job of the day."

"But you didn't go in that night?"

"No, and thank goodness I didn't, otherwise I might have walked in on the murderer."

"Why didn't you go in?"

"I was told not to."

"By who?"

"Thomas Bradley. I was going to get paid anyway, so to be honest I didn't much care. It meant I got to have an early night."

**

It was my own fault. In a moment of madness, I'd told Constance Bowler that I wanted her to recommend an upmarket restaurant. She'd tried to warn me that Poltergeist Nouveau was expensive, but I hadn't realised I'd need to take out a second mortgage: The starters cost more than I'd usually pay for a three-course meal.

I'd arrived a few minutes before eight o'clock, and been guided to my table by a maître d' who looked down his ghostly nose at me.

"Would *madam* care for a drink while she's waiting for her guests to arrive?"

"I'll just have water, please."

"Still or sparkling?"

"Tap."

"Is that all?"

"For now, yes."

"Very well, madam. *Tap water* it is."

My mother arrived five minutes later.

"This was a lovely idea, Jill." She gave me a hug and a peck on both cheeks. "It's very expensive in here, though. You really must let me pay."

"No, this is my treat."

"That's very kind." She studied the menu. "Everything

sounds delicious."

And so it should at those prices.

"Are you ready to order?" The waiter appeared at our table.

"I am." My mother nodded.

"Could you just give me a few more minutes, please?" I said.

"Of course, madam." The waiter moved on to the next table.

"Are you having trouble deciding?" my mother asked.

"Err—yeah." I glanced at the door, just in time to see my father arrive. He spoke to the maître d' who pointed at our table.

"Darlene?"

"Josh?"

They both glared at me.

"Why don't you sit down, Dad?"

"You didn't tell me *he* was coming," my mother said.

"You didn't tell me she'd be here!" My father was red in the face.

"And *why* do you think that was? Because I knew what kind of reaction I'd get."

The two of them sat in silence, eyeballing one another.

"I need both of you to listen to me without interrupting. Do you think you can do that?"

"I can, but I doubt *he* can."

"Rubbish. You're the one who doesn't know when to be quiet."

"That's rich coming from you."

"Stop it, both of you. You'll get us thrown out."

They glanced around, and realised that they were beginning to attract attention from the other customers.

"Sorry, Jill," my mother said. "He gets me so riled."

"Sorry, Jill. She drives me insane."

"Are you ready to order yet?" The waiter was back.

Once we'd placed our orders, and the waiter had left the table, I took the bull by the horns.

"I need you both to listen to me, and I don't want to hear any interruptions from either of you. Okay?"

They both nodded.

"When I was in Spooky Wooky earlier today, I saw Alberto and Blodwyn; they both looked thoroughly miserable."

"Blodwyn told me she was going into town to buy — "

"Dad!"

"Sorry, Jill. Carry on."

"I went over to join them, to find out what was wrong. They're both sick to the back teeth with the way you two are behaving towards one another. And guess what? So am I."

There was silence for a while, and then my mother raised her hand.

"Yes?"

"Is it okay to speak now?"

I nodded.

"Alberto's right. I've been so angry with Josh that I've neglected him."

"Why are you so angry with Dad?"

"Because he walked out on me. On us. Didn't you?"

"I didn't know about the baby, Darlene. You know that."

"Would it have made any difference if you had?" she said.

"I don't know. I'd made some very bad decisions that

had come back to haunt me. I left to protect you."

"Oh right, so you did it all for me?" My mother spat the words. "I should have realised."

Things were beginning to spiral out of control, so I stepped in again, "Please, both of you. Can we just talk about this without it descending into a brawl?"

"Sorry, Jill, but to hear him talk, he makes it sound like he was doing me a favour. The truth is that our relationship hadn't been great for some time before he upped and left."

"I'm not denying that, Darlene. We were a mess, but I never stopped loving you."

Those words seemed to knock the stuffing out of my mother. "You had a funny way of showing it."

"I was a fool. I should never have left no matter how bad things were. I realise that now. If I'm being honest, I'm still angry at myself for walking out like that. That's why I find it so hard to be around you. It brings it all back again. Whether you believe me or not, I've always loved you, Darlene. And I always will."

My mother's bottom lip began to quiver. "Why didn't you tell me this before?"

"I didn't know how to. I'm sorry."

"So am I."

"Thank goodness for that." I sighed. "Does this mean that the two of you will be civil with one another from now on? If not for my sake, for the sake of Blodwyn and Alberto?"

My mother nodded. "I've been so unfair to Alberto. I'm surprised he's stuck around this long."

"Blodwyn deserves a medal for putting up with me." My father managed a smile.

"I have a suggestion," I said. "Why don't we arrange another dinner, but this time for the four of you?"

"I'm game if you are, Darlene," my father said.

"Why not? It can be a fresh start for us. What about you, Jill? You should join us too."

"No, thanks. Tonight was more than enough for me."

The rest of the evening was delightful: The food was delicious, my mother and father got along like a house on fire, and best of all, they refused to let me pay a penny. When the bill came, they insisted on splitting it between them.

That's what I call a result!

Chapter 16

The next morning when I came downstairs, Jack was on his phone.

"That'll be lovely, Mum. Friday it is. Bye, then."

"Your mum?"

"Yeah. She's coming down on Friday afternoon and staying the weekend."

"Just her?"

"Yes. Dad's been invited to visit an old school friend, apparently. We don't have anything planned this weekend, do we?"

"Not as far as I'm aware."

"You didn't mind me telling Mum she could come, did you?"

"Of course not. Yvonne and I are big buddies now."

"Great. I'd better get going. I promised I'd try to get in early this morning."

When I heard his car pull off the drive, I gave Yvonne a call.

"Yvonne, it's Jill."

"Jack's told you I'm coming down, I take it?"

"Yeah, that's why I called. Is anything wrong?"

"Only that I'm worried about you. I heard on the grapevine that Rex Wrathbringer has said he's confident that the mission will be completed within the next week."

"I take it that *I'm* the mission?"

"Yes. From what I can gather, the witchfinders have reported back that they have you in their sights. Have you identified them yet?"

"I think so. A weird couple moved into one of the

houses across the street. I'm almost certain that they're Vinnie and Minnie Dreadmore."

"Do they both have grey hair?"

"I don't know. They wear balaclavas all the time — probably to hide their hair. Yvonne, can you think of any reason why they would need a lot of buckets?"

"*Buckets*? No, why?"

"They bought sixty-seven of them from our local corner shop."

"That is strange, but then I've heard it said that their methods are rather unconventional. What about The Rose? Any sightings of her?"

"None. Look, it would be lovely to see you, but do you really think it's necessary to come down here?"

"Probably not, but I'll feel better if I'm there. Maybe I'll spot something you haven't. And besides, I've told Jack that I'm coming now."

"What about Roy? Why doesn't he come too?"

"He really is going to visit an old school friend."

"Okay, I look forward to seeing you, then."

"Make sure to be on your guard. I take it you're prepared in case the Dreadmores make their move before then?"

"Yeah. I have plenty of Brewflower at hand."

"Good. See you on Friday."

I'd no sooner finished on the call to Yvonne than my phone rang. I assumed she'd forgotten to tell me something, but it turned out to be Kathy.

"Jill. Meet me on West Street in forty-five minutes, would you?"

"Morning to you, too. What's happening on West

Street?"

"You'll see. Don't be late."

"But, Kathy —"

She'd already hung up.

I had to gobble down my breakfast in order to get to West Street on time. Whatever this was, it had better be worth my getting indigestion for.

***

"So? What do you think?" Kathy had a huge grin on her face.

"About what?" I glanced around.

"This!" She pointed to the empty shop. "Welcome to the future Kathy's Bridal Shop."

I peered through the grimy window. "It's going to need a lot of work from the look of it. It's in a good position, though — just off the high street."

"We could have had either of these." She gestured to the shop next-door which was also vacant. "This one is slightly more expensive, but it's virtually on the corner of the high street."

"Are you sure you can afford it? Wouldn't you be better off across town? I imagine the rents over there are a fraction of these."

"They are, but there's a reason for that. The footfall on the high street is ten times what it is over there. Pete's done the maths, and he reckons even on the most conservative estimates, we should be able to afford this place."

"In that case, I'm really pleased for you. How long do you reckon it will take to get it ready to open?"

"I know it looks pretty grim at the moment, but structurally there's nothing to be done. It's just a case of cleaning it up, giving it a lick of paint, and then getting the shopfitters in. We reckon it will take at least three months. We're planning to do all the initial work ourselves to save money. I thought you could help us."

"Me and Jack?"

"I wouldn't expect Jack to help. He must be busy with his own job."

"And I'm not?"

"It'll be fun: the two of us working side-by-side."

"Sounds like a barrel of laughs. Will you be employing anyone to work in the shop once it's open?"

"Initially, probably not. We thought we'd see how it goes, and then bring someone in part-time if we need to."

"Well congrats. I'd better get going. I've got a busy day ahead."

***

On my way into the office, I decided to check out Nailed-It before it opened for business. Just like Deli, it demonstrated little by way of good taste. The window was covered in posters that looked like they'd been designed by someone without even a rudimentary knowledge of graphic design. Lizzie could have made a better job of them. But the centrepiece of the window was a life-size cardboard cut-out, not of Deli, but of Nails. Printed on the cut-out, in Comic Sans font, were the words: Washbridge's Premier Nail Technician.

I'd expected to find Jules in the office, but Mrs V was all

alone.

"Morning, Mrs V. Shouldn't Jules be in today?"

"She's taken a few days off. Have you forgotten?"

"Oh, yeah. I remember now."

"Sometimes I worry about you, Jill."

"I've had a lot on my mind."

"I'm not talking about Jules. I've never known why you put up with that smelly cat, but this is a step too far even for you."

"Sorry?"

"I know some people like to dress up dogs, but I've never heard of anyone doing it with cats."

"*Dressing up*? Err—excuse me a moment, would you? There's something I need to do."

I went through to my office where I found his whiskersness parading around the room.

"What do you think?" he said. "Do I look good or what?"

"Where did you get the tux from?"

"Feline Tux Hire. You obviously weren't going to suggest my being a pagecat to the old bag lady, so I figured I'd better drop a few subtle hints."

"*Subtle*? You call this *subtle*?"

"Did she say anything? Was she impressed? I bet she was."

"She thinks *I* dressed you in that, and that I've lost my mind."

"If you mentioned the pagecat thing to her, she'd realise that you weren't crazy."

"Somehow, I doubt that."

He sighed. "It doesn't look like there's going to be a wedding invite for me, then."

"If it's any consolation, you do look pretty sharp in that."

***

It was time to have another word with Thomas Bradley. All my instincts told me that he knew more about his brother's murder than he was letting on, and that there was a good chance he was in fact the murderer.

He'd readily agreed to meet with me at his office again, so either he really didn't have anything to hide, or as his wife had suggested, he was supremely arrogant. It was time to find out which.

"Have you made any progress?" he asked, after Ruth Foot had brought through coffee for the two of us.

"Not really."

"Oh? I assumed that's why you wanted another meeting."

"Actually, I wanted to press you on a few matters."

"Go ahead. I've nothing to hide."

"Both you and Georgina insisted that Stephen knew nothing of your affair."

"That's right. We were very discreet."

"Not discreet enough, apparently. I have good reason to believe that Stephen *did* know what was going on."

"Who told you that?"

"That's not important. Not only did he know, but I understand that he intended to confront you about the affair on the night he was murdered."

"That's absolute nonsense. Whoever told you that is lying."

"I believe you knew the confrontation was coming,

which is why you told the cleaner not to come in that night."

"More nonsense. I wasn't the one who told the cleaner to stay away."

"She says you did."

"Then she's mistaken or lying."

"Why would she lie?"

"I have no idea, but then I also have no idea why you're wasting my time with these ridiculous questions. Is there anything else? I do have a rather busy day ahead of me."

"No, that's all. Thank you for your time."

This guy was one of the coolest customers I'd ever encountered. Even though I'd practically accused him of murdering his brother, he'd never once lost his composure. When I left, he was just as calm as when I'd arrived.

Had I got it badly wrong about Thomas Bradley?

I wasn't able to dwell on that thought for long because, just as I was leaving the Nexler Building, my phone rang.

"Is that Jill?"

"Speaking."

"It's Scott Bassett from Pooch First."

"Hi."

"First of all, I wanted to say how pleased I am with Barry's photos. They're magnificent."

"Thanks. We thought so. Let's hope the advertisers do too."

"There are no worries on that score. In fact, that's the main reason for calling you. One of my other models was due to take part in a photoshoot for a doggy-bed company today, but the poor lad has come down with a cold. The client has to go ahead with the shoot, otherwise they'll miss the TV slots they've got booked. Anyway, long story short, they'd like Barry to take his place if that's possible?"

"Today?"

"Yeah. I realise it's short notice."

"I don't think we'll be able to manage that."

"The money's good. Six-hundred pounds."

"What time do you need us to be there?"

"In two hours. Can you manage that?"

"Of course. Barry would be devastated to miss out on the chance. Give me the address, and we'll be there."

I magicked myself straight over to Aunt Lucy's.

"Hi, Jill. Thanks for what you did at Cuppy C. The twins were really worried they'd lost their livelihood."

"No problem. By the way, I think you might be right about Grandma turning over a new leaf. She actually praised me for solving the 'softer' spell mystery."

"I told you, didn't I? It's taken long enough, but it looks like she's finally begun to mellow in her old age. Would you like a cup of tea?"

"Not for me, thanks. I'm here for Barry, actually. He's got his first modelling assignment."

"When?"

"In a couple of hours."

"Oh dear."

"What do you mean: *oh dear*?"

"We've just come back from our walk in the park. You'd better take a look for yourself. He's in the back garden."

I hurried through the house, and out of the back door.

"Jill!" Barry, or at least something Barry-shaped, came rushing towards me.

"No! Don't jump—"

Too late. He'd already planted his huge, muddy paws on my chest.

"We've been for a walk, Jill. It was great!"

"Did you go in the lake, by any chance?"

"I wanted to say hello to the ducks."

"You're absolutely filthy."

"I'm sorry about the state of him, Jill." Aunt Lucy had followed me outside. "I tried to stop him, but you know how he is when he gets excited. I was going to leave him out here until he'd dried off, and then try to get him clean."

"There isn't time for that if he's going to make it to the commercial shoot."

"Commercial?" Barry's tail began to wag. "Am I going to be on TV?"

"You were supposed to be."

"Brilliant! Let's get going."

"You can't turn up looking like that."

"Please, Jill. This is my big break."

"Hold on. I've had an idea." I grabbed my phone, and made a call.

***

The woman at Woof Wash didn't bat an eyelid when she saw the state of Barry.

"Thanks for squeezing us in like this. He's in a bit of a mess, I'm afraid."

"No problem. It isn't every day that we get to treat a supermodel."

"That's me, Jill." Barry was barely visible through the

soap suds. "I'm a supermodel."

"Not yet you aren't. Keep still or you won't be ready in time."

"I'm keeping still. Look, I'm like a statue."

Fifty minutes later, Barry looked and smelled like a new dog. I paid the woman, including a generous tip, and then the two of us hurried to Candlefield Lighthouse Studios. We got there just in time for the shoot. I was rather disappointed not to be allowed on set to see Barry in action. Instead, I was forced to kick my heels in reception.

Just over an hour later, he reappeared, accompanied by a young witch.

"Jill? I'm Maddy."

"How did it go?"

"Fantastic. I understand this is Barry's first assignment?"

"That's right."

"You'd never know it. He's a natural. He takes directions really well."

"Does he?" Knowing how difficult it was for me to get Barry to do anything, that came as quite a pleasant surprise.

"Absolutely. He made our job much easier. We'll be giving him good feedback to the agency. He should get plenty of work."

"Thanks." I patted Barry. "Well done, Boy."

"Does that mean I'm a supermodel now?"

"I guess so."

***

After dropping Barry back at Aunt Lucy's, I went over to Cuppy C.

"Look." Amber tapped the counter. "It's not floppy."

"Everything's back to normal then, I take it?"

"Yeah. Including Pearl skiving off again. She's gone shopping with Alan."

"You don't seem too concerned?"

"Nah, I don't mind. William and I will have our turn at the weekend. I'm just pleased the shop is back to normal."

"Does that mean the muffins are on the house for me today?"

"Yeah, I suppose so. *A* muffin, though. Singular."

"Thanks. This is kind of a celebration."

"How come?"

"Barry has just finished his first modelling assignment."

"I bet it was a nightmare."

"Actually, it wasn't. According to the people at the studio, Barry is a natural. They think he'll get plenty of work."

"It's a pity it doesn't pay better. Mum said you'd told her that he'd only make a pittance."

"Err—yeah, that's right. It's barely worth my time really. I only do it for Barry's sake."

"You're a good egg, Jill."

"I do my best."

What? Okay, so I'm a smelly, rotten, bad egg. Satisfied? Sheesh—judgemental or what?

***

My next port of call was the maze at Washbridge Country Hall. I found the Blues Brothers, Bobby and Billy, at the centre of the maze. Until I'd put a stop to their little game, these two had got their kicks from scaring the guests and workers who ventured into the maze.

Bobby Blue had his head under his arm—old habits die hard, I guess.

"What do you want?" Billy said. "We haven't taken any more Spookberry."

"Don't send us back to GT," Bobby's detached head said.

"Relax. I'm not here for you two. I need your help."

"Why should we help you?"

"So that I don't remember what you were up to, and inform the authorities."

"That's blackmail."

"I prefer to call it—err—no, you're right. It is blackmail."

"What is it you want?"

"I need to get hold of Homer Range."

"We don't know where he is."

"I can tell you're lying because your lips are moving. Now, are you going to tell me, or shall I make a call to the GT police?"

"Don't do that," Billy said. "I have his business card; his phone number is on there."

"Thank you, gentlemen. As always, it's been a pleasure doing business with you."

Chapter 17

When I got back, Deli was seated in the outer office, talking to Mrs V. Well, not so much talking *to* her as talking *at* her.

"Hi, Jill." Deli greeted me with a green lipstick smile. "Been out crime-busting?"

"Something like that."

"Annabel and I have been having a good old chinwag, haven't we?"

"We certainly have." Mrs V rolled her eyes. "I was just telling Mrs Lane how busy we are."

"Enough of the Mrs Lane, Annabel. I've told you to call me Deli. Everyone does."

"Of course." Mrs V forced a smile. "I was just telling *Deli* how extremely busy we are. Isn't that right, Jill?"

"That's right. We've got so much work on at the moment that it isn't even funny."

"That's what I thought." Deli stood up. "I said to myself, that young Jill is overdoing it. She needs to take more breaks, or she'll make herself ill. That's why I popped by — for a coffee and a chat." She turned to Mrs V. "Make Jill and me a coffee, would you, Annabel? And bring it through to Jill's office."

Before I could object, Deli took me by the arm, and practically frogmarched me through to my office.

"What's that daft cat of yours wearing?"

"It's — err — well, it's err —"

"It looks like a tux. You're as daft as me, Jill. I used to dress my Cleopatra up like that. She had this beautiful pink coat — all sparkly it was. Did I ever tell you about Cleopatra?"

"Is she the cat you left on the bus?"

"Yeah, that's her. Broke my heart when I lost her, it did. Mind you, the umbrella I got from lost and found is still going strong."

Mrs V brought through the coffee, and made a point of slamming Deli's cup down on the desk—not that Deli noticed.

"You got any biccies, Jill? If I remember right, you were always partial to a custard cream or ten. I bet you have a packet of them in here somewhere, don't you?"

Reluctantly, I fished the half-empty packet out of my desk drawer, and watched in horror as she helped herself to three of them. Three! The greed of some people.

"It's nice that we work so near to one another, Jill. We can have these little chats whenever we feel like it."

"Yeah, but the nail bar does seem to be super busy."

"It is. It's going great guns, but between you and me, there's not a lot for me to do until I get up to speed working on *real* hands. Nails is handling all the appointments at the moment."

"He must get tired? Doing all that by himself, I mean?"

"Nah, he's loving it. It's like he's found his true vocation at last."

Just then, my office door flew open, and Mrs V came charging in.

"Jill. Something terrible has happened."

"Oh, right, okay." I stood up. "Sorry, Deli, I'll have to take care of this."

"No problem. I'll check that Nails is okay. I might as well take the rest of these biccies with me. You don't mind, do you?"

Before I could answer, she'd already grabbed them and made her exit.

"Thanks for rescuing me, Mrs V. I think she would have been here all day."

"I didn't make that up about the emergency. Armi just called me to say he'd heard that a shop on the high street has collapsed."

"What? Which one?"

"I don't know, but I thought you'd want to check just in case—"

I was already on my way out of the door and down the stairs. There were dozens of shops on the high street—the chances of it being Ever were remote, but I was still worried enough to run all the way down there.

The police had already thrown up a cordon at the end of the high street, and they weren't allowing anyone through. The rescue workers were all gathered on the opposite side of the road to Ever. They appeared to be standing close to where Ma Chivers' shop, Yarnstormers, was located. Or at least, where it used to be located.

"What happened?" I asked one of the police officers.

"A shop has collapsed."

"What caused it? Was it a gas explosion?"

"They don't know yet."

"Anyone hurt?"

"It doesn't look like it. Apparently, they received some kind of warning before it collapsed. As far as we know, they all got out in time."

"Thank goodness for that. My grandmother has a shop down there. Can I go and check if she's okay?"

"Sorry. No one is allowed through until the rescue services give the all clear."

I was never going to be able to persuade the police to let me through the cordon, so I found a quiet alleyway, made myself invisible, and then hurried down the street. Just as I'd thought, it was Yarnstormers that had collapsed. Some of the staff were still near to the scene, talking to the police. Fortunately, they all seemed perfectly okay.

"There was a phone call," a young woman said to the police officer who was taking notes. "They said we should all get out straight away because the building was about to fall down. We thought it was a joke at first, but we decided we'd better get out just in case. It's a good thing we did because ten minutes later, this happened."

Across the road, the lights were on in Ever. A number of staff and customers were still inside the shop—presumably because the police had told them to stay put for the time being.

One of the Everettes was standing in the open door, and I just managed to squeeze past her. Everyone was looking through the window, so no one noticed me reverse the 'invisible' spell just before going into Grandma's office. The woman herself was seated with her bare feet resting on another chair. Grossville!

"If it isn't my darling granddaughter. To what do I owe this unexpected pleasure?"

"I heard there'd been an incident on the high street, so I thought I should—err—that I'd better check if you—err"

"How very sweet. You were worried about me. Well, as you can see, I'm perfectly fine, which is more than I can say for Yarnstormers. They seem to have had a spot of bother."

"*A spot of bother*? The shop has collapsed."

"That's very unfortunate, but then there are a lot of old mine shafts running under this area. Or so I hear."

"Wait a minute. Is that what you meant when you said you were going to *undermine* Ma Chivers?"

Grandma said nothing, but her grin gave her away.

"You could have killed someone."

"Don't be so melodramatic. I warned them to get out, and then did a quick check of the building myself before I gave the boys the say-so to finish the job."

"*The boys?*"

She reached down, and picked up a cage, which she placed onto the desk.

"What are those?"

"What do they look like?"

"Moles."

"Well done. Ten out of ten."

"How could those tiny things have done that kind of damage?"

"Come on, Jill. You're supposed to be little miss superwitch. Use your imagination."

"You made them larger."

"Much larger." She cackled.

"You can't go around doing things like this. You've totally destroyed —"

"A competitor. That's right. And don't go feeling sorry for Ma Chivers. Have you forgotten what she did to Cuppy C?"

"What about all of her staff? They're out of a job now."

"They needn't be for long. I've had one of the Everettes pass them a business card with my number on. Now that Yarnstormers is out of business, I may open a wool shop again."

"Are you going to bring back Ever A Wool Moment?"

"Why not?"

"But there isn't room in here. Not now you've extended the tea room."

"It won't be based in this building. I thought it might be nice to build a new shop from the ground up."

"Where?"

"I hear there'll be a nice space across the road when they eventually remove all that rubble. I'll be needing a manager if you're interested."

Unbelievable.

***

I popped back into the office just long enough to let Mrs V know what had happened on the high street. I told her that Yarnstormers had collapsed, and that everyone had got out okay. Needless to say, I didn't mention the part that Grandma had played in it.

"That's terrible, Jill. Thank goodness everyone is okay. I know I shouldn't be thinking about something as trivial as this right now, but this will make things very difficult for the yarnies. First, Ever closes and now Yarnstormers has gone. What will we do?"

"I wouldn't worry about it. I have a feeling that you won't have to wait too long for another wool shop to sprout up."

"I do hope you're right, Jill."

***

When I stopped to pay the fee at the toll booth, it was

Mr Ivers who stuck his hand out for the cash.

"What happened to 'Andy'?"

"My bosses have banned me from using him."

"Why? I thought after the snafu with the rain, he'd been working okay."

"He was. Well, except for that one minor incident."

"What happened?"

"It wasn't Andy's fault. The woman leaned too close to him."

"And?"

"Her scarf got caught on his arm. When it swung back inside, it kind of — well, it wasn't as bad as she made it out to be. I managed to cut her loose before she lost consciousness. She was a bit red in the face, but that's all."

"I don't imagine she was best pleased."

"She reckons she's going to sue the company."

"No more Andy, then?"

"No. My poor elbows are already giving me gyp."

"You should make Cole a better offer to tempt him back."

"I might just have to do that."

***

I was just about to go into the house when I heard Clare, my next-door neighbour, call my name. When I turned around, I was confronted by a giant heart.

"Hi, Jill. Do you like my costume?"

"It's for CupidCon, I assume? Yeah, I really *heart* it."

"Thanks. I managed to nab the last heart in the costume shop. According to the manager there, there's been a run on them this week."

"Because of CupidCon, presumably?"

"No. Actually, most of the people who have hired the hearts are going to CardiacCon. It was silly to schedule them both on the same day if you ask me."

"Is Tony going to CupidCon?"

"I don't know, and I don't care."

"You know very well that I'm going." Tony came out of the house; he was wearing a costume shaped like an arrow. "I wouldn't miss it for the world."

"Tell him I don't care, would you, Jill?"

"Tell her that I don't care if she doesn't care."

"Ask him if Wendy is going to be there."

"Tell her that I haven't seen or spoken to Wendy, would you?"

"Tell him—"

"Sorry, I think I just heard my landline. I hope you both really *love* your con."

* * *

It was my turn to make dinner, so when Jack texted to say he was just about to set off for home, I used the app on my phone to order in pizza.

Isn't modern technology wonderful?

"I thought you were going to make dinner tonight," Jack said when he saw the pizza.

"Did I say that? I could have sworn we'd agreed on pizza. It looks delicious, doesn't it?"

"I guess so. I assume you heard about the shop that collapsed on the high street? When I heard it was a wool shop, I thought it might be Ever, but then I remembered your grandmother had given up the yarn side of the business."

"For now."

"Sorry?"

"It was very bad from what I heard. The whole of the shop collapsed; it will have to be demolished."

"How does something like that happen?" Jack pinched the last slice of pizza just before I was able to grab it. "Mine shafts, I assume."

"That or moles."

"What? Oh, yeah. Very funny. They'd have to be some pretty big moles."

"I saw Tony and Clare on my way in."

"Have they made up yet?"

"Not that you'd notice. They're still not speaking to one another."

"I guess that means they won't be going to CupidCon, then?"

"You'd be wrong. Clare was dressed as a heart, and Tony was dressed as a giant arrow."

"Thank goodness we don't fall out like that."

"We never will because I know you wouldn't cheat on me."

"Because I love you too much?"

"That and the fact that I'd break your legs."

Even though I'd made dinner, I volunteered to do the washing up. That's how big hearted I am.

What? There were at least two plates and two glasses. They weren't going to wash themselves, were they?

"Jill!" Jack shouted from the other room. "Didn't you say you'd been working on a case at the Nexler Building?"

"Yeah, why?" I hurried through to the lounge.

"Look." He pointed at the TV.

Earlier this afternoon, the road outside the Nexler Building was closed while the authorities recovered the body of a man. We understand that he committed suicide by jumping from the roof of the building. Unconfirmed reports suggest that the man was Thomas Bradley, a director of West Star Advertising, who occupy the top floor of that building.

"Did you know him?" Jack asked.

"Yeah. He's the one who hired me to investigate the murder of his brother. I spoke to Thomas Bradley earlier today."

"How was he then?"

"Fine. At least, I thought so at the time. Can you do me a favour, Jack?"

"Do I have a choice?"

"Not really. Would you call one of your old buddies at Washbridge police station, to see if there's any more to the story than they said on the news."

"Okay. I can't make any promises though."

While Jack went upstairs to make the call, I reflected on my meeting with Thomas Bradley. I'd all but accused him of murdering his brother, but he hadn't turned a hair. He'd been so calm that I'd more or less convinced myself that I must be barking up the wrong tree. But now I wasn't so sure. Perhaps, I'd got it right. Maybe, Thomas had decided I was getting too close, and decided to end it all.

Jack came back into the lounge. "I managed to get hold of Grant Grantham."

"And?"

"You mustn't repeat this."

"You know me."

"That's why I said it. Not a word to anyone."

"Okay. I promise."

"There's some suggestion it may not have been suicide. There was a woman up on the roof. She's been taken in for questioning."

"Did they say who it was?"

"The deceased's wife: Georgina Bradley."

Chapter 18

The next morning, I walked into my office building at the same time as Brent from I-Sweat.

"Morning, Jill. We haven't seen you in the gym for a while."

"I keep meaning to pop in, but I've just been so busy. You know how it is."

"Oh yeah." He grinned. "I know exactly how it is. I bet you find time to drop into Coffee Triangle though, don't you?"

"Busted. I'm definitely going to make the effort to drop by the gym at least once a—"

"Day? Week?"

"I was going to say month, but yeah, I'll shoot for once a week."

"By the way, do you still have a cat in your office?"

"Officially no, but between you and me, I do still have Winky. Why?"

"We found one wandering around the gym yesterday. I've no idea how it got in. He's not yours, is he?"

"How many eyes does he have?"

"*Eyes?*" He laughed. "Two, of course."

"It's not Winky then. He only has the one."

"Right. We held onto him in case anyone came by to claim him, but I guess we'll have to take him to the cat shelter."

"What does he look like?"

"Grey. Quite skinny."

"Keep hold of him for one more day, would you? I'll ask around to see if anyone has lost him."

"Okay, thanks."

"When did you put these on my desk, Jill?" Mrs V held up a handful of silver horseshoes, which were decorated with ribbons. "I was beginning to think that you weren't interested in my wedding."

"Of course I am," I lied.

"Where did you get them?"

"I—err—Kathy had a few samples for her shop."

"They're very nice, but I'm not sure about the cats."

"*Cats*?"

"Look, there are small cats printed on the horseshoes."

"I hadn't noticed those."

"Maybe Kathy will get some others I can look at."

"Maybe. I'll let you know."

"So?" Winky was sitting on my desk. "Do I get the gig?"

"If you're talking about being a pagecat for Mrs V, then I'd say you've got two chances: slim and forget it."

"What about the horseshoes? She must have liked those?"

"Why would she want horseshoes with little cats printed on them?"

"I thought they were classy."

"Never mind the horseshoes. I assume you're still running the Midnight Gym next door?"

"You'd better believe it. That's turned out to be a nice little earner."

"I think one of your members may be in a spot of bother."

"What do you mean? Has one of them damaged the

equipment?"

"No. I just saw Brent from I-Sweat. He said they'd found a cat wandering around in the gym."

"Grey?"

"Yeah."

"Skinny?"

"Yeah. How did you know?"

"That's Micky The Mill."

"*Mill?*"

"Tread*mill*. The guy is obsessed with them. I get lots of complaints from the other members because he hogs one of the treadmills for hours on end. He's always the last one to leave. I often have to drag him out before I lock the back entrance."

"It sounds like you might have missed him this time."

"I bet he was hiding so he could grab a couple more hours on the treadmill after I'd locked up. He probably thought he'd be able to sneak out without being noticed when the humans arrived. What an idiot."

"Unless someone claims him today, he's going to end up in the cat shelter."

"There's no one to claim him. Micky's a bit of a loner; he lives on the streets."

"Looks like the cat shelter for him, then."

"We can't let that happen. He's on two-strikes already. If he gets handed in again, it'll be—" Winky drew his finger across his throat. "We have to rescue him."

"*We?* He's one of your members. He's got nothing to do with me."

"Come on, Jill. You wouldn't want to see him sent to the great cattery in the sky, would you?"

"What do you expect *me* to do?"

"Pretend he's your cat and go and claim him."

"I've already told Brent that he isn't."

"Tell him you made a mistake — that you forgot you had two cats."

"That would make me look stupid."

"And your point is?"

"I'm not going to pretend he's my cat, but I think I know how to save him."

"You're a little diamond. Haven't I always said so?"

My phone rang.

"Can I speak to Phil Goodyear?" It was a man's voice. One I didn't recognise.

"Who?"

"My name is Ormerod Longcastle. I represent Mrs Georgina Bradley. She's asked me to contact the P.I. she hired to investigate her former husband's murder. She gave me this number, and the name Phil Goodyear. Are you Mr Goodyear's secretary?"

"It isn't Phil, it's Jill. And it isn't Goodyear, it's Gooder. That's me: Jill Gooder."

"You're a woman."

There were no flies on this guy. "Can I help you Mr Shortcastle?"

"*Long*. It's *Long*castle. She'd like to speak to you. I've told her I don't think that's a good idea, but she insists."

"When?"

"This morning. She's being held at Longdale Prison. Do you know it?"

"Yes, I've been there before."

"Oh?"

"To interview someone."

"Of course. Can you get there for eleven?"

"Yes."

"I'll meet you there, then. I've told Mrs Bradley that I want to be present at your meeting. I trust that will be acceptable to you?"

"No problem. I'll see you there, Ormer — err — "

"Rod."

"Okay, Rod. I'll see you there."

"Hey, where do you think you're off to?" Winky called after me as I headed for the door.

"I have to interview someone in prison."

"What about Micky."

"He'll have to wait."

"What if they take him to the shelter while you're out? Do you really want that on your conscience?"

"Oh, alright then. I'll get Micky first."

I was still trying to figure out how to rescue Micky The Mill when my phone rang again. Probably Roddy and his long castle.

"What now?"

"It's Scott Bassett. Did I call at a bad time?"

"Hi. Sorry, things are a bit hectic right now."

"I was just wondering if Barry would be free to do another commercial tomorrow? This one is for Barkies. Have you heard of them?"

"They're Barry's favourite treat."

"Really? That's good. Will he be able to make it? The pay is the same as last time."

"Definitely. What time do you need us?"

"Eleven-thirty. I'll text you over the details."

"Okay. Great."

Winky was glaring at me. "While you're busy gassing on the phone, Micky might be on his way to death row."

"Shut it. I'm doing the best I can. And anyway, I'm going to need your help."

"Sure. What do you want me to do?"

"I'm going to make myself invisible. As soon as I've done that, I want you to screech as loud as you can."

"Why?"

"I need you to get Mrs V in here."

"Why?"

"There's no time for twenty questions. Just do it. And you'd better make it loud because Mrs V is pretty hard of hearing. Okay?"

"No worries. I've got this."

As soon as I was invisible, Winky let rip like I'd never heard him before. Moments later, Mrs V came through the door.

"Jill? What's going on in—" She glanced around. "I could have sworn she was in here." She glared at Winky. "What's all that noise about? Put a sock in it or I'll feed you one of mine."

That was my cue to slip out of my office. I grabbed Mrs V's coat on my way past her desk, and then once I was out in the corridor, I cast the 'ageing' spell and reversed the 'invisible' spell.

"Hello, there," the receptionist at I-Sweat greeted me. "You must have seen our new ad."

"I don't know what you mean, dear," I said in my old lady voice.

"The promotion we're running for senior citizens. I didn't think the ads ran until next week. Have you brought some clothes to change into?"

"No, I — err — "

"Not to worry. I can still give you a tour of the gym." She came from behind the desk, but suddenly stopped dead in her tracks. When I followed her gaze, I realised why. After casting the 'ageing' spell, I'd thrown on Mrs V's coat, but I was still wearing my high heels.

"I'm not actually here for the seniors' gym, dear."

"Oh?"

"I've lost my cat. He's grey and rather thin. I wondered if he might have found his way in here?"

"Yes, he has. He's in the office. I'll go and fetch him for you."

"Thank you, dear."

She glanced again at my footwear, and then disappeared through the door behind her. Moments later, she reappeared, carrying Micky.

"There you go. It's a good thing you came to get him. We were going to take him to the cat shelter later today."

"Thank you, dear." I took the cat from her. "Who's been a naughty boy?"

"Who are you?" Micky hissed.

"Shut up," I whispered.

"Sorry?" The receptionist looked puzzled.

"Take no notice of me, dear. I live alone so I often talk to him, don't I, Micky?"

"Never seen you before." He eyed me suspiciously.

"I'd better get him back home. Thanks for your help, dear."

Once I was back in the corridor, I reversed the 'ageing'

spell and headed back to the office.

"Jill?" Mrs V looked even more puzzled than the I-Sweat receptionist had. "Why do you have—?"

"You're probably wondering why I have this cat."

"Actually, I was wondering why you have my coat on."

Oh bum!

"I—err—it's a funny story. You'll laugh when I tell you. I was looking through my office window when I saw this little rascal running back and forth across the road. He was nearly run over a couple of times, so I thought I'd better go and rescue him. I was just about to go downstairs when it occurred to me it would be chilly out. I didn't want to waste time going back for my coat, so I grabbed yours instead. I hope you don't mind."

"Err, no, that's okay. I didn't see you take it, though."

"You were busy looking at the horseshoes. Would you mind holding him for a moment, please?" I passed Micky to her. "Just while I slip off your coat."

She pulled a sour face, and held the cat at arm's length.

After hanging up her coat, I took Micky back and hurried through to my office.

"Micky!" Winky yelled. "What have I told you about getting out of the gym on time?"

"Sorry, Winky. I was trying to beat my endurance personal best."

"You're going to get yourself killed."

"It won't happen again." Mickey turned to me. "How did you do that? Back at the gym, you looked a hundred years old, but now you look quite hot."

"Thank you, kind sir."

"Don't go telling her that," Winky said. "She'll be

unbearable. You can put him down now."

As soon as I put Micky down, he hurried over to the open window. "I'll get going then. Thanks, Winky. Thanks, Sexy."

"Sexy?" Winky laughed.

"What's funny about that?"

"He wouldn't think you were sexy if he saw you picking your nose."

"I do not pick my nose."

***

I arrived at Longdale prison ten minutes early, so I made a call to Aunt Lucy.

"It's Jill. I had a phone call from Pooch First earlier. They have another commercial lined up for Barry tomorrow at eleven-thirty. Can you make sure he doesn't get dirty in the morning because I won't have time to take him to the groomers."

"No problem. I'm taking him to the park this afternoon because I've arranged to meet Dolly and Babs, but I'll keep him in tomorrow."

"Thanks. I'll see you then."

A few minutes later, a red Jag pulled up next to my car. I knew it was Longcastle — he had solicitor written all over him.

"Ms Goodyear?"

"It's Gooder. Nice to meet you, Rod."

"It's Ormerod."

"How's Georgina holding up?"

"She wasn't very good when I left her yesterday. The

truth is, Ms Goodyear, things don't look very good for her. I'll most likely be advising her to take a plea."

"Isn't that a little premature?"

"When you've been at this as long as I have, you get a nose for it."

He'd certainly got a nose for it. It was at least two sizes too big for his face.

Georgina Bradley looked terrible, as though she hadn't slept for a week; the prison garb didn't help.

"I'd like to speak to Jill alone, Mr Longcastle."

"I think I should be present."

"I said I'd like to speak to her alone."

"Very well." He snorted.

"Where did you find him?" I asked, once he'd left the room.

"He was appointed for me. I'm going to sack him and get someone else at the first opportunity. Thanks for coming to see me."

"No problem."

"I didn't kill Thomas. He'd already jumped when I got on the roof."

"What were you doing at the Nexler?"

"I got a call to say Thomas wanted to see me urgently, so I jumped straight in the car. When I got to his office, there was a note on his desk, saying he'd gone up onto the roof for a cigarette. I went straight up there, but there was no sign of him. That's when I heard screams coming from down on the street. When I looked over the edge—" She hesitated. "He must have jumped just a few minutes before I got there. I rushed down as quickly as I could, but they wouldn't let me get anywhere near him. Everything's a bit of a blur after that."

"When did they arrest you?"

"Ruth put me in a taxi and sent me home. I was lying on the bed when they came to the door. It must have been about six o'clock. I assumed they'd come to ask me to identify the body, but they arrested me."

"On what grounds?"

"They knew I'd been on the roof at around the same time as Thomas. They say someone in one of the buildings opposite saw a woman push him, but I swear I didn't do it, Jill. I know I said I was going to leave him, but I would never have done anything like this."

"I believe you. What happened to the note that Thomas left on his desk?"

"I left it there. I don't know what to do, Jill, that's why I asked Longcastle to contact you. Do you think you can find out what really happened?"

"Yes, don't worry. Everything is going to be okay."

Back outside, Longcastle was on his phone. When he spotted me, he ended the call.

"I'd like you to brief me on what was said, Ms Goodyear."

"No need. Mrs Bradley asked me to give you a message, Rod."

"It's Ormerod. What's that?"

"You're a waste of space and you're fired."

"What? I've never been so insulted."

"I find that very hard to believe."

He huffed, puffed and then stormed away.

I was just about to get into my car when my phone rang.

"Is that Jill Jackson?"

"Who? Err—yeah, Jill Jackson speaking." I'd almost blown it. Jackson was the name I'd left on Homer Range's answerphone.

"This is Homer Range. I got your message about the Spookberry."

"Thanks for calling back, Mr Range. I'm looking for someone who can supply large quantities of Spookberry, and I was given your name by Bobby and Billy Blue. Can you help?"

"I certainly can."

"Great. In that case, perhaps we could meet at my country house just outside Washbridge if that suits?"

"Absolutely. Just tell me where and when."

Chapter 19

It was Friday and another big payday for yours truly, courtesy of my wonderful, darling Barry. Six-hundred pounds just to sit around for an hour or so while he did his thing. It didn't get much better than that.

What? Of course Barry would get his fair share of the rewards. He could keep all of the Barkies they gave him today. I can't say fairer than that, can I?

First though, I was going to call in at the Nexler Building, to see the concierge, Lucas Broad.

"Morning, Jill. If you were intending to go up to West Star's offices, there's no one up there. They've closed for the rest of the week out of respect after what happened on Wednesday. I assume you heard?"

"About Thomas? Yes. In fact, I went to see Georgina Bradley in Longdale prison yesterday."

"I can't believe she did it. She always seemed such a nice lady."

"I'm not sure she did. That's why I'm here this morning. Would you have time to take me through the CCTV footage for Wednesday."

"Sure. I'll ask Joe to take over here, and we can go to the control room."

"I'm not sure how useful this is going to be," he said, once we were in front of the computer. "You do realise there are no cameras on the roof, don't you?"

"I didn't. That's a bit of a blow."

"There's coverage of Georgina arriving at the building, and then again when she got out of the lift on the top floor. Wait, I'll show you." He tapped the controls until he had the required footage on screen. "There, that's when she came into the building. And that's when she reached the top floor."

"Is there footage of her going through the door that leads to the roof?"

"No. There isn't a camera there either, but there is footage of her when she comes back downstairs. Wait, I'll just find it for you. There it is."

I leaned forward to get a better look. The expression on Georgina's face was one of horror. Either she'd been traumatised by what she'd just seen, or she was an amazing actor.

"Okay, Lucas, thanks."

"While you're here, do you want to take a quick look at the CCTV coverage from the day Stephen Bradley was murdered?"

"I'm not sure there's much point now."

"It'll only take a few minutes if I whizz through to the important bits."

"Okay, why not?"

He slipped the DVD into the computer, and pressed fast-forward. After a couple of minutes, he slowed it down to normal speed. "That's where Ruth Foot leaves the building."

"Okay."

Fast-forward again.

"That's Thomas Bradley leaving."

"Right."

"And that's Stephen on his way to the toilet."

"I take it that's after Thomas had left?"

"Correct. There's nothing else to see really." He pressed

fast-forward again.

"Hold on. Who's that?" I pointed to a figure, wearing a blue tabard, walking towards the entrance to the building.

"That's the cleaner."

"I thought she hadn't come in that night."

"She came in but was sent away again. Watch."

The woman, who had her back to the camera, entered the building. Fifteen minutes later, she came back out, and disappeared off-camera.

"I don't understand. Who told her that she wasn't required?"

"I assume Stephen Bradley must have. He was the only one left in the office."

"Could I borrow this DVD?"

"Sure."

I didn't want to say anything to Lucas, but the CCTV footage didn't match up with what Josey Wilde had told me. Or maybe I'd just misunderstood. To clarify matters, I called her, but she was in a meeting, so I asked if they'd get her to call me back as soon as she was free.

***

It was time to collect Barry, my little money-making machine. When I arrived at Aunt Lucy's, she was packing stuff into boxes.

"You look busy."

"I'm packing things ready for the move."

"That won't be for weeks yet, will it?"

"No, but I thought I could make a start with some bits and pieces we won't be needing before then."

"Is Barry upstairs?"

"He is, but there's a slight problem."

"Don't tell me you let him get dirty again."

"No. He's lovely and clean."

"What's wrong then?"

"I think it would be better if he told you himself."

I didn't like the sound of that, so I hurried upstairs.

"Are you ready to go and shoot another commercial, boy?"

"Don't want to go."

"What? Why not? I thought you liked being a supermodel."

"Don't want to do it anymore."

"Tell me why."

"Just don't."

"Oh, for goodness sake." Hamlet sighed. "Apparently, his lady friend doesn't like him appearing on TV."

"Is that true, Barry?"

He nodded.

"Why not?"

"She says I'll get lots of admirers, and then I won't want to be her boyfriend anymore. It's not true. I would never leave Babs, but she said if I don't give up the modelling, she'll dump me."

"Don't worry about her. There are plenty more dogs in the sea."

"Not like Babs. I don't want to lose her."

"Why not just do this one. It's for Barkies. They're your favourite."

"Not doing it."

"I could step in for him," Hamlet volunteered. "Just look at this magnificent profile." He turned side on.

"Thanks for the offer, but I don't think that's going to work."

"I take it you weren't able to change his mind?" Aunt Lucy said when I got back downstairs.

"I can't believe it. I thought he loved the idea of being a supermodel."

"Not as much as he loves Babs, apparently."

"I guess I'll have to tell Pooch First to take him off their books."

"Oh well, never mind. It's not like they paid very much anyway, is it?"

What do you mean, it served me right?

* * *

Long after I arrived back in Washbridge, I was still feeling sorry for myself. All that money lost and for what? Puppy love.

My phone rang; it was Josey Wilde.

"I have a message to call you."

"Thanks, Josey. I just wanted to check something with you."

"Okay."

"When you said that you hadn't cleaned on the night of the murder, I assumed you hadn't gone to the building at all."

"That's right."

"So, just to be absolutely clear. You didn't show up and then get sent away?"

"No. I got a phone call, telling me not to come in."

"And it was Thomas Bradley who phoned you?"

"Actually, it was his PA. She told me Thomas had said I shouldn't bother coming in."

"Ruth Foot?"

"That's right."

The mystery thickened.

Back at my office, Winky was standing on his front paws, with his back paws resting up against the wall.

"Dare I ask what you're doing?"

"What does it look like?"

"It looks like you're standing on your head, but why?"

"It's for the brain."

"How does that help your brain?"

"It improves the blood flow. You should give it a try."

"I think I'll pass."

"Your loss."

I had much more important things to do than stand on my head. I had a murder, possibly two, to solve, and I needed to get Georgina Bradley out of prison.

I tried to put the DVD that Lucas Broad had given me into the slot on my computer, but there was already something in there, so I pressed the eject button.

"Hot Cats Do Yoga?"

Winky rushed across the room, leapt onto the desk, and snatched the DVD.

"Have you been watching naughty movies on my computer?"

"No, of course not. It's — err — an instructional DVD. I'm learning yoga."

"Why: *Hot Cats*?"

"Have you ever tried yoga? It really takes it out of you. That's why they're hot."

"A likely story."

After he'd slunk off, I slipped my DVD into the slot, and fast-forwarded until I reached the part where the 'cleaner' entered and then soon after left the building. The woman had her back to the camera all of the time, as though she knew she was being filmed. Unable to see her face, I was about to give up, but then I spotted something.

I zoomed in to take a closer look, and bingo!

I made another call to Josey Wilde; this time she was at her desk.

"Sorry to bother you again, Josey."

"No problem."

"Do you remember the uniform you wore when you used to clean at West Star?"

"It wasn't exactly a uniform. At least, not like the ones my staff wear now. I just used to dress in a blue tabard. They were cheap and nasty—I used to go through a lot of them."

"Is it possible you could have left one at West Star's offices?"

"I might have done. Occasionally, I'd arrange to meet up with friends on a Friday night after I'd finished at West Star. I used to take a change of clothing with me to save time. It's possible I might have left a tabard behind. Why?"

"No reason. Thanks very much. That's been very helpful."

Although Georgina Bradley was being held in Longdale prison, she was only on remand, which meant she was allowed more visits and phone calls than someone serving time. I'd called the prison, posing as her new lawyer, and requested to schedule a phone conversation with her. Just under an hour later, that phone call came through.

"Jill? Is that you? They said you were my new lawyer?"

"I may have bent the truth a little. Listen, this may sound like a strange question, but what were you wearing when you went to the Nexler Building on Wednesday?"

"My grey suit. Why?"

"Were you still wearing it when you were arrested?"

"No. When I got home after finding Thomas dead, all I wanted to do was get into bed and go to sleep. I threw the suit over a chair — it's probably still there."

"So, the suit is still at your house?"

"I suppose so. When the police came to the door, I just threw on a pair of jeans and a top. Why do you want to know about the suit?"

"I'll explain later. Thanks, Georgina. Hang on in there."

***

By the time I'd been to Georgina's house and then rushed back to the Nexler Building, where I executed the first part of my cunning plan, I was exhausted. Unfortunately, there was no time to rest because, before I embarked upon the final part of my cunning plan, I had a meeting to attend at the colonel's old house.

As arranged, the colonel and Priscilla were there to let me in. After wishing me luck, they went back to Ghost Town. Ten minutes later, there was a knock at the door.

"Mr Range?"

"Do call me Homer. And you must be Jill Jackson."

"That's me. Please come in."

"This is a beautiful house. Have you lived here long?"

"I married Horace shortly after moving to Washbridge from Candlefield."

"Is your husband a human?"

"He is indeed. Anyway, beautiful as this house may be, it's very costly to maintain. We've been looking for ways to generate some additional income, and I thought ghost tours might be just the ticket."

"And for that, you'll need ghosts."

"Precisely. The problem is that the regular ghost-hire agencies want to charge an arm and a leg."

"That's very true."

"In the course of my research, I realised there was a much cheaper way of doing this. I could simply bring in my own ghosts, but to do that I'll need a supply of Spookberry. As luck would have it, I read about the 'hauntings' over at Washbridge Country Hall, so I took a trip over there, and got talking to Bobby and Billy. They were the ones who recommended you."

"If it's Spookberry you want, I'm your man."

"Excellent, but are you able to supply it regularly in large quantities?"

"Absolutely. I can get as much as you want whenever you want it."

"That's great. Why don't we go through to my office, and we can talk prices?"

"Happy to."

As soon as we walked through the door, two GT police officers grabbed him by the arms.

"What's going on?" He tried to break free, but one of

the officers slipped a pair of handcuffs around his wrists.

Constance Bowler stepped forward. "Homer Range, I'm arresting you for the illegal supply of Spookberry Potion."

"You can't prove a thing."

"I think you'll find I can." She produced a digital recorder from her pocket, and played back the conversation that Homer and I had had a few minutes earlier. It was a little muffled, but loud enough to be obvious that it was Range's voice.

He was still protesting his innocence when the two officers took him back to GT.

"Thanks, Constance," I said.

"Not at all. I should be thanking you. His arrest should put a severe dent in the trade in illegal Spookberry."

***

Ruth Foot lived alone in a bungalow located ten minutes from Kathy's house. She looked surprised to see me.

"I hope you don't mind my calling on you like this. I didn't phone because I was in the neighbourhood anyway, visiting my sister. She lives just down the road."

"Did you want to come in?"

"Yes, please."

"Can I get you a drink?"

"No, thanks. I wouldn't want to take up any more of your time than I need to."

She led the way through to the lounge.

"I called at your offices, but they're closed."

"We thought it only right given what happened to Thomas."

"Of course. What will happen to the business now?"

"I'm not sure. That will be up to the other shareholders, I guess."

"I assume the main shareholder is now Georgina. Maybe she'll decide to continue the business."

"I'm not sure she'll be in a position to do that. Didn't you hear that she's been arrested for Thomas' murder?"

"I did. In fact, I went to see her in prison."

"How is she?"

"Buoyed by the fact that she's likely to be released any time now."

"Really? I thought they had a witness who saw her push Thomas?"

"The witness saw a woman push him, but they were too far away to identify her. That won't matter anyway because the CCTV captured what actually happened."

"There aren't any cameras up there."

"There weren't until last week. The management company had one installed, to monitor for people smoking on the roof." I took out my phone. "I viewed the footage earlier, and took a copy. Look." I pressed 'Play'. "See, that's Georgina. Notice how there's no one else on the roof when she appears. Watch her reaction after she's looked over the edge. Do you see that?"

Ruth said nothing, so I continued, "See how Georgina rushes back to the door. Can you see the look of horror on her face?"

Ruth continued to stare at the screen, but still said nothing.

"Would you like to see the earlier footage? The part where Thomas comes onto the roof, followed by you. He's so busy enjoying his cigarette, and looking out over the rooftops that he doesn't realise you're behind him until it's too−"

"Stop!" She tried to knock the phone from my hand.

"The police will be here in a few minutes. Is there anything you'd like to tell me before they get here?"

Her tears began to flow. It was several minutes before she was composed enough to speak. "I was in love with Stephen. He said he loved me too."

"You were having an affair?"

"That makes it sound sordid−it wasn't. Stephen promised that when the time was right he'd divorce Georgina and marry me. I was patient−very patient. I waited and waited, and then when I found out that Georgina was seeing Thomas, I thought our time had come. When I told Stephen, I was sure that he'd leave her, but−" Her words trailed away.

"What happened, Ruth?"

"He said he could never leave Georgina. He said that he and I had been *fun* while it lasted, but that it could never amount to anything."

"Did he say he was going to confront Thomas that night?"

"Stephen?" She managed a sour laugh. "Of course he didn't. He was too much of a coward. He said he was going to talk to Georgina, to try to convince her to end the affair. He said he'd do whatever it took to save his marriage, starting with ending our relationship. Just like that. Then he said it would be best if I left the company."

"So, you decided to kill him?"

"He'd destroyed my life. He'd said he wanted us to be together, but then discarded me like a piece of garbage."

"You contacted the cleaner and told her not to come in.

Then, after you'd made sure the CCTV had caught you leaving the building, you returned dressed as the cleaner. You stayed just long enough to kill Stephen."

She laughed. "You should have seen his face. He wasn't laughing after the first blow. Or the second."

Confession over, Ruth dissolved into tears. She was still crying ten minutes later when Susan Shay and her team arrived.

Chapter 20

My little ruse had worked even better than I could have hoped.

To create the bogus CCTV footage, I'd used magic to make myself look like Georgina Bradley. Then, dressed in her grey suit, I'd used my phone to film myself on the roof of the Nexler Building. Although I say so myself, my performance had once again been Oscar worthy.

My only concern had been whether or not Ruth Foot would buy the story of the new camera on the roof. Fortunately, she was aware that the management company had threatened to take action to combat the smokers, so she'd found the idea credible. That's why when I'd showed her the footage of 'Georgina' on the roof, she'd assumed it was genuine.

Next had come the *big bluff*. I'd asked if she wanted to see the earlier footage which would show her pushing Thomas off the roof. If she'd said 'yes', my cunning plan would have been scuppered because, of course, no such footage existed. Luckily, my hunch had proved to be correct: She'd been taken in by the fake footage, and had no desire to witness herself committing murder. Instead, she'd begun to sing like a bird.

Needless to say, Susan Shay had been her usual, ungrateful self. Had she bothered to thank me for solving two murders? Of course not. After arresting Ruth, she'd given me the usual lecture about keeping my nose out of police business.

Sushi? That woman could kiss my— You get the picture.

***

Who deserved coffee and a muffin?

That's correct: I did.

While on my way down the high street towards Coffee Triangle, I heard someone call my name. When I turned around, I saw Ma Chivers headed my way. Her face was bright red, and something told me she was not a happy bunny.

"Did you really think you could get away with this, Gooder?" She gestured to what was left of Yarnstormers.

"I didn't have anything to do with that."

"You're a liar. I know you and your grandmother were behind it. I also know that you were the one who shut down my spell battery operation."

"You mean the spell batteries that you used to put Cuppy C out of action?"

"I don't know what you're talking about. I was running a perfectly legitimate business."

"Of course you were. Just how stupid do you think I am?"

"You won't get away with this. Either of you."

"You talk a good game, Ma, but that's all it is. You're all talk."

"Think so, do you? You ought to ask your new friend, Alicia, if she agrees."

"What do you mean? What have you done to her?"

"Me? Nothing, of course." She cackled. "Like you just said, I'm all talk." She turned away. "Be seeing you, Gooder."

I tried Alicia's number, but there was no reply. Was Ma

Chivers bluffing or had she really done something to her? I wasn't Alicia's biggest fan because she'd once tried to kill me, but more recently, she'd distanced herself from Ma Chivers, and had been instrumental in helping me to resolve the 'softer' spell incident.

I genuinely hoped she was okay.

***

Something strange was going on in Coffee Triangle. Normally, as soon as I walked through the door, my ears were assaulted by the sound of whichever instrument was the flavour of the day. Today though, the only sound to be heard was that of conversations from the small number of customers seated at the tables.

"Morning. What can I get for you?" The young woman behind the counter was new, or at least I hadn't seen her before.

"Morning. A blueberry muffin and a caramel latte, please."

"Coming right up."

"How come no one has an instrument today?"

"Haven't you heard? We're about to undergo a major rebranding."

"What does that entail?"

"Coffee Triangle won't be Coffee Triangle anymore."

"What will it be?"

"I'm afraid that's top secret."

"Will you still have instruments?"

"That much I can tell you. We're done with the instruments. In fact, we've been giving them away all week. We might have a few left if you'd like one?"

"Okay. Why not?"

She handed me the coffee and muffin. "I'll just check in the back to see what we have left."

I wasn't sure how I felt about the rebranding of Coffee Triangle. Although the noise could sometimes be a little overwhelming, I'd kind of grown accustomed to the quirkiness of it all. Still, a tambourine or maracas would serve as a reminder of the old place.

"These are all we have left." The young woman held up half a dozen triangles. "Which one would you like?"

"Err — no, thanks. I don't think I'll bother."

"There's no charge. They're free."

"It's okay. I — err — I already have a triangle at home."

I took a seat at a table next to the window, and was just about to take a bite of muffin when Dougal Andrews, reporter for The Bugle, plonked himself in the chair next to mine.

"I don't recall inviting you to join me."

"You try to hide it, but I know you have a soft spot for me, Jill."

"Did you want something, Dougal?"

"I thought you might have some information for me. A little bird tells me that you've been involved in the Bradley murders case."

"No comment."

"I'll take that as a 'yes'. I understand that Georgina Bradley has been charged with her husband's murder. Is it true that she also killed her first husband, Stephen?"

"No comment."

"Come on, Jill. Throw me a bone here."

"Okay, but you didn't hear this from me."

"Of course. My word is my bond."

"It would be wrong for me to name names, but I can tell you that the same woman committed both murders."

"I knew it!" He grinned. "I can see the headline now: Georgina Bradley - The Black Widow. This will show Susan Hall who's top dog at The Bugle."

"How is Susan doing? She came to see me a while back."

"The woman's an amateur. She wouldn't know a good story if it bit her on the bum. She wastes most of her time with nutters who think we've been infiltrated by vampires and the like."

"Really? That's crazy."

"I know. Any time we get a nutter through the door, telling stories about disappearing wizards and the like, we send them Susan's way." He stood up. "I'd better be going. I want to catch the press."

"See you, Dougal. I look forward to reading your article."

Snigger.

***

Back in the office, I was feeling pretty pleased with myself for having solved the Bradley murders.

"You should get married to that human of yours," Winky said.

"Where did that come from?"

"I was just thinking: The old bag lady might not want me as her pagecat, but when you get married, you won't be able to refuse me."

"Want to bet?"

"Come on. We're practically family, and you've seen how good I look in a tux."

"And how exactly would I explain the fact that I'd chosen a cat to perform pageboy duties? They'd call the men in white coats to take me away. And besides, this is all academic because Jack and I have no plans to marry."

Thankfully, this insane conversation was interrupted when my phone rang.

"Jill? It's Georgina Bradley."

"Where are you?"

"Still in Longdale, but they say I should be out within a couple of hours, and it seems that I have you to thank. I can't believe Ruth did it."

"You heard, then?"

"Yes. My new lawyer—my real one—came to tell me what had happened. Apparently, Ruth has been charged with both murders. According to him, she's confessed."

"That's right. She'll probably spend the rest of her days behind bars."

"How did you know she was the one who killed Stephen?"

"I got lucky. Everyone had told me that the cleaner was asked not to come in that night, but when I checked the CCTV footage, I saw a woman wearing a blue tabard go into the building, and then leave shortly afterwards."

"How come no one else picked up on that?"

"They most likely assumed the cleaner had arrived only to be sent away again. In fact, when I spoke to Josey Wilde, she told me that she hadn't gone to West Star at all because she'd received a phone call, telling her not to."

"From Thomas?"

"No. From Ruth Foot. She told Josey that Thomas had

said she wasn't needed that night."

"How did you know the woman in the CCTV was Ruth?"

"I couldn't see her face because she'd deliberately avoided the camera. What gave her away was that ugly ring of hers. Once I realised it was her, everything else slotted into place."

"Why though, Jill? Why did she kill Stephen?"

"You're going to hear this sooner or later, so you might as well hear it from me. When you and Thomas were having an affair, Stephen was seeing Ruth."

"I don't believe it. He would never do something like that."

"He did, but when he found out about you and Thomas, he was determined to win you back. He ended his relationship with Ruth, and told her she'd have to leave her job. I guess she just flipped."

"Poor Stephen. He should have left me; it's what I deserved. If he had, he'd probably still be alive. Why did she kill Thomas?"

"When Ruth found out that you and Thomas had asked me to re-investigate the murder, she panicked. After all this time, she'd probably assumed she'd got away with Stephen's murder. Now there was a possibility that she might still be found out, so she decided to take you both out of the picture. Ruth knew Thomas's routine; he took his cigarette breaks at the same times every day. She followed him onto the roof, and pushed him off. But first, she called you, and left the note for you to find. Once you were on the roof, she disposed of the note, then sat back and waited for the police to arrest you. With Thomas dead and you in prison, she assumed she'd be safe."

"How did you manage to get her to confess?"

"I simply confronted her with what I believed had happened, and she cracked. I guess the stress of trying to keep her secrets finally caught up with her. I was just lucky."

"Lucky or not, you saved my skin. I can't thank you enough."

"No thanks necessary."

"You'll send me your bill, I assume?"

"It'll be in the post tonight."

***

Jack had arranged to collect his mother from the railway station at six o'clock. I'd made sure I was home by three, so I could give the house a good clean before she arrived.

What? Of course I used magic. I had my nails to think of.

It had just turned three-thirty when my phone rang.

"Jill, it's Yvonne."

"Hi. Is everything okay?"

"Yes, fine. I took an earlier train, so you and I can have a chat before Jack gets home from work. I've let Jack know he doesn't need to collect me."

"Okay. What time does your train get in? I'll come and pick you up."

"No need. I'm already in Washbridge. In fact, I'm in a taxi, and should be with you in a few minutes."

"Okay. See you soon."

Five minutes later, there was a knock at the door.

"Good afternoon, Jill."

"Blossom?"

"I'm really sorry to trouble you, but I've just realised I'm out of sugar. I don't suppose you have any I could borrow, do you? I'd go to the corner shop, but my leg has been giving me gyp these last few days."

"Sure, no problem. Wait there and I'll go and get you some."

I left her at the door, and made my way into the kitchen. I knew we had an unopened bag of sugar somewhere, but where? I tried the cupboard closest to the window.

"Any last words, Gooder?"

I turned around to find Blossom, standing in the kitchen doorway. Her voice had changed; it was much deeper than usual. But that was the least of my concerns. The look on her face was one of sheer hate. Gone was Blossom, the little old lady. In her place stood someone I now realised was The Rose.

I'd been such an idiot. I'd been so focussed on the balaclava twins, convinced that they were Vinnie and Minnie Dreadmore, that I'd never given the sweet old dear from across the road a second thought.

"Well, Gooder? Surely, the most powerful witch that has ever lived must have something to say before you die?"

The Brewflower was in my handbag in the lounge. Why hadn't I kept some in different locations around the house? Because I was an idiot; a complacent idiot. Soon to be a dead idiot.

"You don't have to do this, err—what do I call you? Blossom? The Rose? Thorny?"

"I'd heard that you thought you were something of a

comedian."

"I do my best. Anyway, before you do your thing, don't you want the sugar?" I launched the bag at her.

She ducked to one side, which gave me a chance to rush past her. My magic couldn't hurt her, but if I could get to the Brewflower, I might still have a chance.

I made it into the lounge, but before I could grab my handbag, she shouted, "Too late, Gooder." She was standing in the doorway. "It's time for you to die."

It was all over. I'd planned to leave Jack, but I hadn't expected it to happen like this.

Goodbye, Jack, my love.

"Stop!" Yvonne shouted.

The Rose spun around; that gave me the opportunity to grab my handbag, and take out two syringes of Brewflower.

The scream made my blood run cold.

When I looked up, I saw the elderly witchfinder, standing over Yvonne's prone body.

I rushed over, and slammed both syringes into The Rose's neck, causing her to stagger out into the street. I could probably have stopped her getting away, but I was much more concerned about Yvonne.

"You'll be okay. I'm going to call an ambulance."

"It's too late." She grabbed my hand. "Promise that you'll take care of Jack."

"I — err — I —"

"Please, Jill. You have to promise."

"I promise."

Moments later, the light disappeared from her eyes, and she stopped breathing.

"Yvonne! Please, no! Yvonne!"

Chapter 21

"I'm off, Mrs V."

"Okay, dear. I'll be leaving soon myself. I just want to finish this pair of socks for Armi." She held up her knitting.

"Red and green stripes? Nice."

"His favourite colours."

"Before you go, Jill, I wanted to ask how Jack is doing."

"Better, thanks. Much better."

"What about you? These last few weeks can't have been easy for you either."

"I'm okay."

"Are you sure? You've been pretty quiet."

"Honestly, I'm fine, but I'd better be making tracks. Goodnight."

"Goodnight, dear."

It was just over a month since Yvonne's death. Naturally, Jack had been devastated by his mother's sudden and untimely demise. I'd done my best to console him, but it hadn't been easy because I'd been racked with guilt. The official cause of death had been listed as a heart attack — only I knew the truth: Yvonne had died saving my life.

My stupid secret had killed his mother and was now putting Jack's life at risk; that was unacceptable.

As Yvonne lay dying, she'd made me promise that I'd take care of Jack. There was now no doubt in my mind that the best way to do that was to put an end to our relationship. I still loved him just as much as I ever had, but that was irrelevant. All that mattered now was his safety.

He would be devastated when I told him, but I couldn't afford to let that change my mind. Everyone would think I was cold-hearted, but there was nothing I could do about that. All that mattered now was that I distance myself from Jack in order to keep him safe.

Now wasn't the time to tell him, though. I would have to wait until Jack was strong enough to take another blow. How long would that be? Three months? Six months? A year? I had no idea, but until that time arrived, I would somehow have to carry on as though everything were fine.

***

Aunt Lucy now had the keys to her new house, and I'd promised to go with her to help measure up for curtains. To be honest, I wasn't really in the mood, but I didn't want to let her down.

I was just about to magic myself over to Candlefield when my phone rang; it was Kathy. Over the last few weeks, she and Peter had been like rocks for Jack and me. This was probably her regular call to make sure I was okay.

"Jill, are you in the office?"

"I just left. I'm on my way to the car."

"I'm sorry to bother you, but would you have a minute to come down to the shop?"

"Now?"

"If you can."

"What's it about?"

"It'll be easier to show you."

"Okay. I'll be there in a couple of minutes."

As I made my way down the high street, I could see Kathy waiting for me on the corner.

"Hi, sis." She gave me a big hug. "How are you?"

Much as I appreciated the concern that both she and Peter had shown us over the last month, I was actually looking forward to the time when Kathy and I could revert to our normal sisterly relationship: the one in which we spent most of the time sniping at one another.

"I'm good. What's up?" I glanced through the window of Kathy's soon-to-be shop.

Over the last couple of weeks, she and Peter had been working on it every spare moment they had, but from the look of it, they still had a lot of work to do.

"Haven't you noticed?"

I looked again to see if I'd missed something, but nothing leapt out at me. "Noticed what?"

"Next door."

The shop adjoining Kathy's had been let a few days after she'd signed the lease for hers, but as far as I could see, the interior of that shop still hadn't been touched.

"What about it?"

"Up there." She pointed.

I hadn't noticed the brand new sign which read: ForEver Bride.

"When did that go up?"

"I don't know. It wasn't there when I left yesterday. They must have put it up overnight."

"Why would someone open another bridal shop, right next door? Surely the owner must have enquired what kind of shop you were planning to open?"

"You've missed the important part. Look again at the

name."

"Forever Bride? It's quite catchy. Maybe you should have a rethink about yours to see if you can come up with something more —"

"You're still missing the point. Look at the word 'Ever'. It should have a small 'e', but it's capitalised."

"So what? People often —" And then the penny dropped. "Hold on. You don't think — she wouldn't, would she?"

"Of course she would. It's exactly the kind of thing your grandmother would do. When I told her about my plans, and how we thought we'd spotted a gap in the market, she'd seemed genuinely interested. No wonder. She must have been planning how she could make her own move into the bridal business. I never dreamed she'd stoop so low as to open up right next door to us."

"There are no depths to which Grandma won't stoop. What are you going to do?"

"I'm not going to let anyone, and especially not your grandmother, wreck our plans. If she wants a fight, she's got one."

Whilst I admired Kathy's determination, she had no idea what she was up against. Competition was one thing, but there was no way it would be a level playing field. Grandma had one thing that Kathy didn't: Magic. You only had to look at what she'd done with the wool shop: products such as Everlasting Wool and One-Size knitting needles had simply destroyed the competition. Who knew what kind of magical innovations she had planned for the bridal shop.

"Is it worth it? Wouldn't you be better locating somewhere else, or opening a different kind of shop?"

"And let her win? I'm surprised to hear you suggest that, Jill. You've never let anyone walk all over you. Why should I? And besides, the lease has been signed, and I've already placed orders for the initial stock."

"Maybe I could have a word with her. I might be able to get her to change her mind about the shop."

"Some chance of that." Kathy laughed. "But if you do speak to her, you can give her a message from me. Tell her: This is war."

Oh boy.

***

Aunt Lucy was waiting at the door of her 'old' house. She looked as excited as a young child with a new toy.

"Did you remember to bring a tape measure?" I asked.

"Yes. And a notepad and pencil. Will you drive, Jill?"

"Sure. Aren't the twins coming with us?"

"I asked them, but they've got a couple of people off with the flu, so they couldn't get away. To tell you the truth, I'm glad it's just the two of us. You know what they're like—we'd never get anything done."

"That's true."

"How are you and Jack bearing up?"

"We're okay, thanks."

"I know you blame yourself for what happened, but it wasn't your fault. You didn't force Yvonne to come over to your house."

"That doesn't make it any better. Whichever way you look at it, if Jack and I weren't an item, Yvonne would still be alive."

"That's silly talk. Yvonne did what she did because she

wanted the best for her son. And that's you."

Although Aunt Lucy meant well, her words were no comfort at all. Yvonne's death had been my fault—plain and simple. If I'd told Aunt Lucy of my plans to leave Jack, she would have tried to talk me out of it, so I didn't intend to say anything until the deed was done.

The interior of the new house looked larger now that most of the furniture had been removed. All that was left were the few pieces that Aunt Lucy had agreed to buy from the previous owner.

"I love buying curtains, don't you, Jill?"

"Oh yeah. It's one of my favourite things."

"That's a good sign." She grinned. "You must be getting back to your old self."

"What do you mean?"

"The sarcasm. I've missed it."

"Oh, right." I forced a smile. "When will you be moving in?"

"Lester has booked next Wednesday off."

"Will you need a hand?"

"It's okay. We've booked Were Removals."

"Werewolves, I assume?"

"Yes. Those guys will make short work of it. You must come over and see us as soon as we're in."

"Don't worry. I'll be here. Just make sure you stock up on the custard creams. By the way, have you seen anything of Grandma today?"

"No. She was out before I was up and about this morning."

"I need to have a serious word with her."

"What has she done now?"

"I can't be certain, but I think she may have taken the vacant shop next door to Kathy's new bridal shop."

"Why? What's she going to use it for?"

"That's just it. If I'm right, she's planning to open a bridal shop too."

"What makes you think it's your grandmother's?"

"The name. It's called: ForEver Bride, and the word 'Ever' has a capital 'E'."

"It might just be a coincidence."

"Do you really believe that?"

Before she could answer, there was a loud thud.

"That came from next door, didn't it?" I said.

"I think so. I noticed the 'For Sale' sign had been taken down the last time we were here."

Another thud.

"It sounds like you have new neighbours."

"Let's go and say hello."

"They might be busy."

"Nonsense. It's never too early to get to know your new neighbours. Come on."

Aunt Lucy led the way next door. The door was open, so she knocked, and called out, "Hello! Anyone in? We're your neighbours."

Moments later, there was the sound of footsteps.

"Hello there, neighbour," Grandma said.

"Mother?" Aunt Lucy looked stunned. She wasn't the only one.

"Do you have any tea at your place, Lucy? I haven't managed to bring any supplies over yet."

"Mother?"

"Why do you keep saying that? Do you have tea or not?"

"What are you doing here?"

"I live here. Didn't I mention I'd bought this place?"

"No, you didn't. When did you buy it?"

"When you told me you were moving, I decided to checkout your new house, and what can I say? I fell in love with this place. So, it seems we're still neighbours. Isn't that nice? Now, about that tea? Do you have any?"

"Err—yes. I brought some over yesterday."

"Good. Off you trot, and put the kettle on while I show Jill around my new house."

Still stunned, Aunt Lucy went back next door.

"How could you do this, Grandma?"

"Do what?"

"Buy this house without telling Aunt Lucy?"

"You mean like she bought her house without telling me?"

"That's different."

"Are you coming in or what?"

I followed her into what was an almost carbon-copy of the house next door. After she'd shown me around, I decided to tackle her about the shop.

"Grandma, is that your shop on West Street?"

"You've seen it, then?"

"Why would you open it right next door to Kathy's bridal shop?"

"Is that what she's opening? I'd totally forgotten."

"Don't lie. You know very well that's what she's doing."

"A little competition is a healthy thing."

"Fair competition, maybe, but how can she compete if you use magic like you did in Ever A Wool Moment?"

"I'm sure she'll find a way."

"You're right—she will. Because I'm going to help her. If you use your magic to give yourself an unfair advantage, then I'll do the same thing for Kathy."

"That sounds like fighting talk."

"You'd better believe it."

"I look forward to it. Now, shall we go and get that tea?"

***

When I arrived home, Jack's car was already on the drive. He'd been finishing work early more often recently. Although he'd never actually said as much, I'd got the impression that his mother's death had made him rethink his work-life balance.

As soon as I walked through the door, I could hear him laughing. Not something he'd done a lot of recently.

"Jill? Come and look at this."

I found him seated on the sofa, laughing at something on the TV.

"What are you watching?"

"Look. Do you recognise those two?"

A man and a woman were being interviewed. They both had long hair: the man's was dyed red, the woman's was bright green.

"No, but they look a right couple of weirdos."

"Look closer. Try to imagine them without hair."

I took another look. "I've never seen them before."

"I'll give you a clue: buckets."

"What are you talking—hold on—it can't be."

"It is. It's the balaclava twins."

The so-called balaclava twins had lived across the road

from us for a short while. They were weird with a capital 'W'. They always wore balaclavas, and never spoke to anyone. But their main claim to crazy was that they'd purchased the entire supply of buckets from The Corner Shop — all sixty-seven of them. Until The Rose had struck, I'd been convinced they were the witchfinders, Vinnie and Minnie Dreadmore.

"What are they doing on TV?"

"Apparently that's Chris and Chrissie Chrisling — better known as Chris To The Power Of Three."

"You are joking."

"I'm not, and if you weren't such a philistine, you'd know they were world famous artists."

"No way."

"Yes way. Just wait until you see their latest masterpiece. There, behind them."

"What is it?" I got as close to the TV as I could. "Are those — ?"

"Buckets? Yes. They call the piece Pail Imitation. Get it? Pail?"

"It's rubbish. It's just a few buckets stuck together in a heap."

"To you and me, maybe. To art connoisseurs, it's an important piece, which is expected to fetch over three million pounds."

"You're having a laugh."

"That's what they reckon. Not a bad return for buying a few buckets. It's a pity we didn't think of doing it."

"I still don't understand why they were living across the road."

"In their interview, they mentioned they'd been living incognito, so that they could work without the eyes of the art world on them."

"Why the balaclavas?"

"I assume they were afraid they might be recognised. Their hair is quite distinctive."

"Recognised? Around these parts? I can't imagine there are many art aficionados in Smallwash. Anyway, it's nice to see you laughing, even if it is at those two nutters."

He gave me a kiss. "Come on through to the dining room. I've made dinner."

"That's the best crockery. What's the occasion?"

"You'll see. Sit down. Dinner is almost ready."

Before I could ask any more questions, he disappeared into the kitchen, and returned with a roast dinner for each of us.

"That looks lovely, but I'd still like to know what this is all about."

"Eat up before it goes cold. All will be revealed later."

Jack was happier than I'd seen him since before his mother's death. I can't remember what we talked about over dinner. It was nothing deep—just the type of idle chat we used to indulge in.

"That was delicious, thank you," I said after we'd finished dessert. "You have to let me do the washing up."

"Don't worry, I intend to, but first there's something I want to ask you."

"Okay."

He fished around in the pocket of his jacket, which was on the back of the chair.

I saw the ring even before he'd got down on one knee. From that moment on, everything seemed to happen in slow motion.

"I love you, Jill Gooder, and I want to spend the rest of

my life with you. I want us to have children together. Will you marry me?"

I could barely see for the tears streaming down my face.

When I didn't reply, he said, "I was hoping you wouldn't have to think about it. You must have been expecting this."

At that moment, I hated that I was a witch. If I'd been just a normal human being, I would already have said 'Yes', but how could I? But if I said 'No', it would crush him.

"I want to, but—"

"But what?" He stood up. "I love you. I know you love me. What's the problem? Don't you want us to spend the rest of our lives together? Don't you want us to have children together?"

"More than anything."

"Say you'll marry me, then."

"I can't. Not while—"

"While what? Jill, tell me."

"There's something you don't know about me."

"Whatever it is doesn't matter." He hesitated. "You're not already married, are you?"

"No, of course not."

"What is it then? I guarantee it won't change the way I feel. Tell me, please."

"Okay. You deserve that much." I wiped the tears away. "You'd better sit down because it's a long story, and you're probably going to think I'm crazy."

"I already think that." He grinned.

"It started about two years ago when I got a phone call from my birth mother."

"I didn't think you knew your birth mother."

"The first time I saw her was on her deathbed. She contacted me because she had something important to tell me before she died. I got there just in time, and with her dying breath, she said I was a witch."

"What? I'm sorry to say this about your mother, but to ignore you all of your life, and then to use her last breath to insult you? She must have been a nasty piece of work."

"That's what I thought at the time, but it wasn't meant as an insult. She was telling me something that I needed to know. I really am a witch."

He said nothing for a few moments, but then laughed. "You had me going there for a minute. I thought you really did have some deep, dark secret that you were scared to share with me."

"I'm not joking, Jack. I realise how crazy it sounds, but it's true, and I'm going to prove it to you."

"Okay." He was still grinning. "I'll play along. How exactly do you intend to do that?"

I cast the 'shrink' spell to make myself six inches tall, and then looked up at him and said, "How's this for starters?"

ALSO BY ADELE ABBOTT

The Witch P.I. Mysteries
(A Candlefield/Washbridge Series)

Witch Is When... (Books #1 to #12)
Witch Is When It All Began
Witch Is When Life Got Complicated
Witch Is When Everything Went Crazy
Witch Is When Things Fell Apart
Witch Is When The Bubble Burst
Witch Is When The Penny Dropped
Witch Is When The Floodgates Opened
Witch Is When The Hammer Fell
Witch Is When My Heart Broke
Witch Is When I Said Goodbye
Witch Is When Stuff Got Serious
Witch Is When All Was Revealed

Witch Is Why... (Books #13 to #24)
Witch Is Why Time Stood Still
Witch is Why The Laughter Stopped
Witch is Why Another Door Opened
Witch is Why Two Became One
Witch is Why The Moon Disappeared
Witch is Why The Wolf Howled
Witch is Why The Music Stopped
Witch is Why A Pin Dropped
Witch is Why The Owl Returned
Witch is Why The Search Began
Witch is Why Promises Were Broken
Witch is Why It Was Over

Witch Is How... (Books #25 to #36)
Witch is How Things Had Changed
Witch is How Poison Tasted Good
Witch is How The Mirror Lied
Witch is How The Tables Turned
Witch is How The Drought Ended
Witch is How The Dice Fell
Witch is How The Biscuits Disappeared
Witch is How Dreams Became Reality
Witch is How Bells Were Saved
Witch is How To Fool Cats
Witch is How To Lose Big
Witch is How Life Changed Forever

Susan Hall Investigates
(A Candlefield/Washbridge Series)

Whoops! Our New Flatmate Is A Human.
Whoops! All The Money Went Missing.
Whoops! Someone Is On Our Case.

AUTHOR'S WEB SITE
http:www.AdeleAbbott.com

FACEBOOK
http://www.facebook.com/AdeleAbbottAuthor

MAILING LIST
(new release notifications only)

http:/AdeleAbbott.com/adele/new-releases/

Printed in Great Britain
by Amazon